"I'm none the worse for sleeping alone," Jess said

She held the post steady while Raitt shoveled soil around it. "And I'm still as plain as I've always been. Not the stuff of any man's dreams."

Raitt vigorously tamped down the dirt with his bootheels. "You're not beautiful inside, where it counts, Jess? You're not filled with female desire?"

Jessica let go of the post and suppressed a momentary yearning to welcome his gruff overture. He was the man of her secret dreams, but acknowledging her romantic longings would give him too much power over her.

He caught her gloved hand in his. "Answer me, Jess."

"Let go of me, Raitt."

Tightening his grip, he pulled her close and brushed a string of kisses along her cheekbone.

"Damn you, Raitt," she whispered, surrendering to the sensation.

"That's it, Miss Jess," he said approvingly, letting go of the shovel and pushing back his hat brim. "Cuss me and kiss me."

Roseanne Williams's lastest book involves a vibrant, independent heroine who's an expert with horses. Although Roseanne can't say the same about herself, she went riding *once*. She proudly claims she wasn't thrown from the saddle, but admits, "I ached for days." Roseanne is more interested in another aspect of ranch life—cowboys. "Cowboys have always held a mystique for me," she explains. So it's no surprise that Raitt Marlow, the hero in *Mail Order Man,* is at home on the range. Don't miss Roseanne's next Temptation novel, #460 *Hot Date,* coming in September 1993!

Books by Roseanne Williams

HARLEQUIN TEMPTATION

MAIL ORDER MAN

ROSEANNE WILLIAMS

Harlequin Books

TORONTO • NEW YORK • LONDON
AMSTERDAM • PARIS • SYDNEY • HAMBURG
STOCKHOLM • ATHENS • TOKYO • MILAN
MADRID • WARSAW • BUDAPEST • AUCKLAND

Published May 1993

ISBN 0-373-25543-8

MAIL ORDER MAN

1

"JESSIE-GAL, you need a man."

Jessica Patton stopped washing breakfast dishes and half turned from the sink. She gave her grandfather a look as reproachful as his remark had been. It wasn't the first time he'd spoken those words. He nagged on the subject like a blowfly pestering a horse.

"*You're* a man," she replied. "Why do I need another one if you and I can still handle this ranch without full-time hired help?"

"I'm wearin' out, gal," Dunc Patton persisted. Sitting at the kitchen table, he rocked back in his sturdy pine chair. "Can't tote a hay bale, can't break a horse, can't do half the cattle ranchin' I could do just last year. I need replacin'. Nothin's gonna stop the march of time."

Lying under the table at Dunc's feet, his two Border collies, Murph and Muttley, made growling sounds, as if agreeing with every word he said.

"Granddad, don't," Jessica pleaded gently, a catch in her throat. She turned back to the sink and ran hot water full blast into a cast-iron frying pan. "You're all the help needed here for years to come."

Keeping her eyes on the view through the window above the sink and away from her grandfather, she prevented his piercing hazel gaze from detecting any hint of tears. She looked out at a long, highland valley, bordered by the heavily timbered slopes of the Warner Mountains. This northeast corner of California was isolated, sparsely populated, hospitable only to wildlife, horses, cattle, and hardy ranchers like Dunc and herself.

"Honey, I'm talkin' more than help in your case." Dunc swigged black coffee from a thick, white mug and thumped the cup down on the red-checked, plastic tablecloth. "I'm talkin' a *husband,* dammit. You're past thirty years old. You got a long future you're refusin' to think about. Lot longer than the future I'm lookin' at for myself."

He'd be seventy soon, but Jessica couldn't emotionally acknowledge the fact. She didn't think he looked that old, except for his wiry, white hair. And his shoulders seemed only slightly less broad and burly than when she'd been three years old, riding high on them around this same kitchen table.

But if she turned to look at him again, she knew she'd see his hand tremble involuntarily when he raised his cup to his lips. She'd see age spots on the backs of his square, callused hands, and bifocals perched on his strong nose.

Duncan Patton couldn't possibly grow old, she thought vehemently. He was so dear to her. Dearer than this ranch and the big, pine log house they shared. Fifty years ago, he'd built the house with virgin timber from the surrounding mountain slopes. She would inherit the ranch from him someday, but couldn't stand to think about it yet.

"Your own future isn't as short as you make it sound at the unripe age of seventy," she retorted, moving to the table to wipe up toast crumbs.

"Unripe," he echoed with a snort of disdain. "I'm past ripe, have been since Lizbeth died." He gazed into his coffee, as if seeing his late wife looking back at him. He sighed, a lonesome sound.

Then he looked up, bristly brows drawn together in a frown. "Speakin' of futures, gal, how long's your childbearin' future, huh? Four, five years, at best?"

Feeling her cheeks tint in response to his blunt inquiry, she turned away and brushed the toast crumbs into the soapstone sink. "A husband and children aren't on my wish list at this late date."

"They could be if you'd advertise for a man. A mail order man."

"I already did." She turned and gave Dunc a challenging stare over her shoulder. "Remember?"

"Sure do." He rocked back his chair against the log wall of the kitchen and gentled his tone. "You placed a personal ad just one time in *Ranch Roundup*, honey—and I had to force you into it."

"You saw the men it attracted, Granddad. Three of life's biggest losers, all of them jobless. They each took one look at me and—"

"And what did they see?" he cut in. "You met 'em at the door in boots and jeans and your faded old work shirt, lookin' like Annie Oakley—and smellin' like a horse blanket."

"How else should I look or smell? I ride herd almost every day. They saw that I'm as plain as a fence post, Granddad. It shows, and we both know it."

"A dress and two dots of lipstick wouldn't have hurt," he grumbled. "You might have perfumed your wrists and let your pretty black hair down, or at least tied a ribbon round that ponytail you wear night and day."

Jessica made a face at him. "I'm a working woman on a working cattle ranch. My mail order men weren't interested in mending my fences or kissing my calluses."

"A couple of local yokels've looked twice your way." He paused, then added, "Besides that cowpunk bastard, Budd Cochran, I mean."

"Bastard is too kind a word," she said, scrubbing hard at a stain in the sink. "Like Budd, they've been married and divorced twice or more. I'm better off by myself than getting stuck with what's left out there."

Dunc shook his head. "You're not cut out to live like a nun any more than I'm meant to live like a monk. You're missin' the joy of love and marriage. So am I."

"I'm not missing my independence, Granddad. How many women can say they do exactly what they want without answering to someone? I can. A husband would cramp the freedom I have to be my own woman. He'd fence me in, one way or another."

"Not the right man, gal."

"My eye. Name one man who wouldn't wish I was pretty—or rounder or skinnier or bigger in the bust, longer in the leg. Name him."

"Me. I loved Lizbeth as she was, and I love you as you are."

"Yet you wish I had primped for those three losers."

"Hmph," Dunc said; it was his standard response whenever his half of an argument broke down.

Relieved to have won the point, Jessica picked up a flour-sack towel and dried her hands, then tucked a stray wisp of hair into her ponytail and regarded her grandfather across the table. He could be just as stubborn as he was lovable.

Sighing loudly, Dunc pushed his chair back and stood. "Well, then," he said, "*I'll* place an ad. A body livin' up here with just horses and cattle and two no-place cow towns has to put out word that it's available."

"Granddad, I'll cancel any ad as soon as you place it, so don't bother."

"Easy, gal. I'm sayin' I'll advertise for a wife. None of the widows at church strikes my fancy."

Stunned, Jessica blinked. "A . . . wife?"

"Yup. I still love Lizbeth as much as ever, but after four years alone, I'm heart-deep lonely for a good woman's love. I've got love to give, too. You wouldn't mind some housekeepin' help, would you?" He swiped at a cobweb that dangled from the wagon-wheel chandelier above the table.

"Well, no, but . . ."

"I'll place me an ad then, and see what comes of it."

CALIF RNCHR, WWM, 69 yrs old seeks wife. Photo pls.

Duncan Patton's one-line ad brought three hundred letters in a single month. Jessica came away from the mailbox every day with a handful of perfume-scented responses. Muttering to herself in disbelief, she walked the quarter-mile, dirt driveway back to the house. It was appalling, she thought, that almost half of the letters were from women younger than she was.

One came from as far away as Paris, France. And the explicit photographs some women sent!

When the flow finally dwindled to a trickle, Dunc spread the photos of the most promising candidates on the breakfast table and got out the forked willow branch he always used when he dowsed for well water.

Jessica sat at the table observing him, her emotions mixed. She loved seeing Granddad so cheerful and optimistic again. But how disappointed he would be—as she herself had been—when his respondents traveled to meet him and turned out to be far less suitable for ranch life than their eager, expectant letters implied.

"I should've dowsed those three letters you got," Dunc said, holding the forked ends of the branch lightly in his hands. "We'd have known to run your ad more than once."

"Once was enough," Jessica muttered darkly.

Eyes closed, Dunc instructed her to shuffle the twenty-five photos on the table. She did so, certain he wouldn't blindly locate a wife the way he located underground water. She had seen him dowse for well sites with uncanny accuracy. But pinpoint a wife the same way? Only in his dreams.

"They're rearranged, Granddad."

Without opening his eyes, he began passing the forked branch above the rows of photos. Jessica watched the free end of the branch quiver on its slow journey over each smiling face. Dunc hadn't selected any woman younger than sixty-five. A few were beautiful, most were average, the rest quite plain.

Suddenly the stick dipped toward one snapshot as if an unseen hand had yanked it down.

"Well," said Dunc, opening his eyes, "who's the lovely lady?" He set the branch aside, positioned his bifocals on his nose and sat down in his pine chair to study the picture. "Oh, Evangeline Marlow from San Francisco, is it? Good. I liked her letter best."

He smiled at Evangeline's photo. "She's got a lot in common with me, y'know. Both of us married right out of high school. Both of us widowed now."

Jessica studied the picture and saw an average-looking, pleasingly plump woman, whose fluff of gray hair framed a heart-shaped face. Evangeline's eyes were dark and snappy above a warm, straightforward smile.

Dunc began to read aloud from part of Evangeline's letter. "'I grew up on a Texas cattle ranch, but left Texas when I met and married my late husband. Ours was quite a happy marriage, and I've been very lonely since Leland died almost five years ago. My son and daughter are grown and busy with their lives. I'm free of responsibilities and look forward to getting acquainted with you, should that be your wish, too. Oh, and I prefer to be called Vangie.'"

"She sounds very nice," Jessica murmured, trying not to think of Grandma Lizbeth, who had been the nicest woman in the world.

Dunc nodded. "I've had a special feelin' about Vangie Marlow all along." He pushed the other photos and letters aside. "I'll write my regrets to these other ladies after I put a letter to her in today's mail. I'll give my phone number and tell her to call here collect if she likes what I write."

"She's the only one you're going to contact, Granddad?"

"Yup." Dunc grinned smugly and patted the dowsing rod. "Old Twig here's never failed me yet."

VANGIE MARLOW CALLED long-distance on the evening of the day she received Dunc's letter. Dunc carried the phone into his bedroom and closed the door, keeping Jessica in suspense for two hours.

Trying to watch TV until he finished, Jessica heard Dunc laugh several times during the long conversation. She hadn't heard him laugh like that since Lizbeth's death. Though his laughter was muffled by the closed door, it sounded happy, eager, almost boyish.

She crossed her arms over her chest and frowned at the screen. None of the phone calls from the three lost souls who'd answered *her* ad had made her feel happy, eager or girlish. Their visits had been brief disasters. In fact, the last time she'd felt eager and happy had been . . .

Her frown deepened into a dark scowl as she remembered back that far. Ten years ago. What a fool she'd been to think that Budd Cochran, Dunc's hired hand at the time, had any interest in her, besides adding one more notch to his bedpost! He'd reached his goal after three straight months of the smoothest sweet talk she'd ever heard from a man. The *only* sweet talk she'd ever heard from one.

Dunc and Lizbeth had warned her against Budd, but she had been certain he loved her. The day after he seduced her, he skipped town and never returned. She'd thought her heart was broken—until she overheard in town that he'd done it solely to win a bet with his pals at the corner tavern.

Jessica still burned with humiliation; after all, she had once been the oldest virgin any ranch hand could name at the time, old enough—unattractive enough— to be the subject of a crude, cowboy bet.

Hearing Dunc's door open down the hall, she pretended to be totally engrossed in the "Gunsmoke" rerun. Sheriff Matt Dillon was quick-drawing his gun against a cowpoke villain who bore a skunky resemblance to Budd. "Air-condition him head to toe,

Matt," she urged grimly. When Dunc entered the living room, she pretended to be startled.

"Vangie's comin' to visit here for a couple of weeks," her grandfather announced, his craggy features alight with excitement. "She'll drive up from Frisco, she says."

"Weeks?" Jessica echoed doubtfully.

Chuckling, Dunc settled into his big, cowhide armchair. "We had a fine talk. Two weeks should decide us on each other. She wants to bring a sort of chaperon along. I said anyone she brings is fine by you and me. Right?"

"Of course, but . . ."

"We'll have to get two bedrooms spruced up before they get here late Saturday afternoon," he continued.

"Granddad, that's barely two days from now."

"Yup. The way I see it, Vangie's room will be the one right across from mine." He winked. "Her chaperon can sleep next door to you, and you two'll share your connector bathroom between yourselves."

Jessica wanted to warn him not to let his hopes soar. Hadn't he noticed what rotten luck she'd had with her own ad?

Dunc was setting himself up for crushed hopes, she thought, yet she held back from saying so. He hadn't looked this excited and full of life since before Lizbeth died. He had a sparkle in his eye, and a toothy grin lit up his face.

He must have noticed her dubious expression. "Don't go worryin', gal. This old dowser knows what he's doin'."

She bit her lip and sighed. So much would have to be done before Saturday. All for nothing.

KEEPING WATCH through the front screen door at sunset on Saturday, Jessica saw a cloud of dust roil up where the driveway joined the main road.

"They're here," she called to Dunc, who was tending to a Texas-style barbecue behind the house. Granddad had migrated to California from Texas fifty years ago, she reflected, but there was still as much Lone Star State as Golden State in him.

A speed demon was wheeling up the driveway, she observed, tracking the plume of dust that was heading toward the house. Judging by her letter, Vangie Marlow hadn't seemed the type to drive mountain roads at breakneck speed.

Dunc came up behind Jessica for a look at the dust cloud. "Must be them. Right on time. I closed the dogs in the stable, so they won't make a fuss."

Jessica turned to face him. Dressed in a Western-cut plaid shirt, starched blue denims and dress boots, he looked both handsome and excited. He smelled of Old Spice after-shave and barbecued beef ribs.

"You look great, Granddad."

"You, too," he said, giving her shoulders a quick squeeze. "All prettied up in a pink dress, see-through stockings and high heels. Hair down from that ponytail and curlin' at the ends." He sniffed the air above her head. "Smell good, too, like a corsage."

"You're making me sound like Cinderella at the ball," she murmured self-consciously. Femininity, beauty and charm were her weak points, as Granddad well knew. She knew just as well how he'd reply. He didn't disappoint her.

"You got a special beauty of your own inside you, gal," he said. "Your prince will come."

Ordinarily, Jessica would have rolled her eyes. She would have muttered that no prince was coming and that there were only toads like Budd in the world for her. But dressed and curled and perfumed to make a good impression on Mrs. Evangeline Marlow for her grandfather, Jessica basked in the love light shining in his eyes. For a brief moment, she felt as lovely on the outside as Dunc always insisted she was on the inside.

The growly purr of a powerful engine grew distinct, then the car glided into view. It was sleek, racy and fire-engine red.

"One of them imported X-Q-Z cars," Dunc observed, adjusting his bolo tie. "Sounds like a herd of wild mustangs under that long hood there."

The low-slung car was grossly unsuitable for mountain ranch life, Jessica was thinking. Judging by her sports car, Mrs. Marlow'd be too merry a widow to live isolated on a northeastern California ranch. She'd be turning back home before Dunc's barbecue came off the grill.

Too bad that her letter and snapshot hadn't hinted at her taste in automobiles. She had looked so average and sensible on paper.

Dunc stepped onto the long, wide porch and waved. Jessica lagged behind him, shading her eyes against the setting sun. Poor Granddad. He'd taken so much trouble with the barbecue, and had spent hours yesterday gathering wildflowers for the guest bedrooms.

She had arranged the flowers in crockery vases for him. After helping her get the guests' rooms ready, he had polished his boots for hours. All for nothing.

Squinting to see against the sun, Jessica felt almost desolate on Dunc's behalf. Old Twig had finally failed him. He should have used it to kindle the barbecue.

The car came to a screeching stop in a backlit billow of dust. Jessica sneezed once, twice, three times. Dunc handed her his handkerchief and blessed her when she sneezed yet again.

The driver's door opened. Seeing a Stetson hat emerge first, Jessica lowered the handkerchief, blinked, caught her breath and shaded her eyes again to see better. The passenger appeared to be a woman, but the driver was clearly a man.

Silhouetted by an aura of setting sun and swirling dust, he stood over six feet tall. Jessica stared, but was unable to see his face beneath the low hat brim. There was only a luminous outline, a virile contour of broad shoulders, slim hips and long legs.

She tottered on her heels, transfixed by the glowing image. Here was the mythical cowboy of her most secret fantasies and dreams! Right here, home on the range.

Dunc sent her a look and raised one grizzled eyebrow. "Well, danged if it ain't a prince."

2

"HOWDY. You must be Raitt Marlow, Vangie's grandson. I'm Dunc Patton."

Raitt swept his Stetson off his head, glad to be free of the hat his grandmother had made him wear to make a good first impression on the Pattons.

He shook Dunc's hand. "A pleasure to meet you." He kept his facial expression polite, but let his handshake transmit his disapproval of his grandmother's visit.

"Pleasure's all mine," Dunc assured him, glancing through the car windshield at Vangie and breaking into a big smile. "I'll give the lady a hand out of your car, if that's okey-doke with you."

Raitt nodded, but still didn't quite smile. He'd once stalked a serial killer who had targeted victims in Personal ads. It was a good thing his grandmother had invited him along on this ridiculous fishing expedition. If she hadn't, he'd have invited himself, to make sure she wasn't anyone's next victim.

Dunc Patton looked decent enough. His handshake was a firm, manly bone cruncher, but Raitt was reserving judgment. Police work had taught him that first impressions were often misleading or entirely false. People proved their personal worth over time.

Dunc Patton would have to prove himself worthy of Evangeline Marlow.

Raitt looked at the woman poised on the top step of the porch. So this was Dunc's tomboy granddaughter. Not quite what he'd been expecting. He recalled how Vangie had vaguely, blithely led him to picture a preteen hoyden with freckles and pigtails. He could see now that his grandmother had been both subversive and purposeful.

"Raitt Marlow," he said, offering his hand. "You're Jessie, I'll bet."

He saw her clench her fingers and twist them around the handkerchief she held. A flush, darker than her shell-pink sundress, was rising up her neck to her cheeks. She was either painfully shy or furious. Furious, he decided, seeing her strong chin jut out and her sage-green eyes flash.

He clearly wasn't what she had expected Vangie's companion to be. No doubt Dunc had been just as vague and blithe as Vangie, and had implied that the chaperon would be female.

"How do you do, Mr. Marlow," she responded, stiffly descending the wooden porch steps and touching only his fingertips before withdrawing her hand. On the bottom step, she caught her left heel in a knothole and pitched forward out of her shoe.

"Ahh!" she exclaimed, going down. "Damn!"

Raitt caught her in his arms. He felt the soft impression of her breasts on his chest, the firm curve of her waist in his grip, the silky sway of her black hair against his cheek. He breathed in her perfume—gardenia—and held her just a little closer than necessary. She wasn't beautiful—not even pretty—but she smelled as exotic and alluring as a hothouse flower.

Shocked speechless, Jessica stared into Raitt's eyes and discovered that they were morning-glory blue. His rescuing embrace felt strong and steely, yet as deep and dreamy as a tropical sea. His body felt overwhelmingly male, giving her the feeling that she was in the grip of a power far greater than she could withstand.

She pushed herself away, jerked backward out of his arms and accidentally knocked his hat from his hand. "Klutz," she muttered at herself.

Raitt bent and freed her shoe from the step. "Are you hurt?"

"No." She stepped back on her bare foot and winced at the pain that shot through her ankle.

"Step light when you're wearin' escalator heels, gal," Dunc advised, coming around the car with Vangie on his arm. "Meet Vangie here while you're still in one piece."

"Hello, Jessie," Vangie said with a warm smile. "Are you certain you aren't hurt? Raitt happens to know first aid and every emergency procedure in the book."

Jessica returned Vangie's brisk handshake and tried to take another backward step without wincing. Pain made her grimace against her will.

Raitt pointed the shoe he held toward the bottom step behind her. "Sit down there. I'll take a look at your ankle."

"No, I'm—"

"Sit, gal," Dunc commanded gruffly, pressing her down onto the step. "Do what the prince—I mean, the man—says. Let him figure out if you're sprained or splintered, while I show Vangie the layout of the house."

"From the outside alone it's magnificent," said Vangie.

"Built the whole place myself, includin' the barn and stable out back," Dunc proclaimed proudly, leading Vangie inside. "Felled every log, mortared every fireplace stone. You like a big, cracklin' fire on a cold winter's night, Vangie?"

Burning with humiliation, unable to walk, Jessica heard their voices fade away. Alone with Raitt, she would now have to submit to his emergency exam.

"This isn't at all necessary," she assured him tartly.

He knelt in front of her and took her foot into his hands. "Wiggle your toes."

Teeth gritted, she wiggled them. "Wearing a pair of boots instead of these damned heels, I'll be just fine," she told Raitt.

"Not for a day or two," he countered, "if you've sprained it."

Jessica tried not to look at his fingers gently probing the bones of her foot and ankle. She tried to ignore how intimately he moved one hand higher, to her calf, her knee. A pleasure sharper than the pain speared through her.

"Any tenderness here?"

"Of course not. I don't have a tender bone in my body, Mr. Marlow. I ride herd, mend fence, cultivate calluses—and detest being set up, the way I see you and I are being set up by our respective grandparents."

"The name is Raitt," he said. "Do you mind being called Jess?"

"No." Budd Cochran had once called her that, and she had minded a lot because it had sounded so hissy. Yet it sounded seductive, coming from Raitt.

"What's in a name, after all?" she added, as much for her own benefit as his.

He nodded in agreement. "Well, I'm not overjoyed to walk into a setup either, Jess. And I have a few calluses of my own to compete with yours."

Jessica was well aware of that; his workworn fingers and palms were snagging her sheer stocking as he felt up and down her lower leg. His careful, searching exam was making her feel bone weak, light-headed and peculiarly female. She wished she could jump up and regain her dignity by marching proudly away from him, into the sunset. She had never fallen headlong off this porch before. Never!

"How have you earned your calluses, Raitt?" she inquired testily.

"The same way you earn yours, Jess. Hard work."

"Doing what?"

"Enforcing the law as a mounted patrol officer, San Francisco Police. Horse cops clean tack and muck out stables as well as ride. But for a week now, my unit's been on involuntary leave due to budget cuts—temporary leave, we hope."

One more unemployment statistic, Jessica reflected. But Raitt's situation sounded less desperate than the hard-luck stories her three mail order suitors had told. She noticed that his hat, more than his clothes, inspired the cowboy image that had mesmerized her at first sight. He wasn't dressed in buckskins or chaps, but in twill slacks and a blue, button-down shirt with the cuffs rolled halfway up his forearms.

She guessed that the hat had been Vangie's idea, much as her own dress and perfume had been Dunc's.

With Raitt's head so close, she could see how thick and deeply golden his hair was. Above his blue eyes, his eyebrows were a shade darker. His nose appeared to have been broken, not unattractively so. His square jaw and firm chin looked unbreakable. He was gorgeous.

Jessica thought of how she looked. Not gorgeous. Not pretty. Not seductive or feminine or shapely, sensuous things males desired in females.

No. She had grown from a tomboy into an active, practical woman who could ride and rope with the best, wrangle a small herd of purebred cattle, and lead a common-sense life without a lover or a husband. No man or woman had ever been more at home on the Western range than she was.

"Something smells pretty nice," Raitt commented softly.

Jessica nodded, sniffing the air. "Texas barbecue is Granddad's specialty. Grilled beef ribs, chili and—" She broke off when Raitt looked into her eyes. Curls of warmth spiraled from where his fingertips touched, all the way up her leg. His gaze was as steady as a blue flame in still air.

"I meant the perfume you're wearing, Jess. Pretty nice."

"I never wear perfume," she stated, hearing her voice almost croak the words. "Tonight is an exception. Only to make a good impression for Granddad." God forbid that Raitt should think it had anything to do with *him*. "Any other time, I smell of horse sweat and saddle soap. I never wear dresses, either, or hose or high heels or—"

She broke off again. Raitt was sliding one arm under her knees and the other behind her back and lifting her against his broad, hard chest.

"Your ankle needs ice," he said, "and you need a softer spot to sit while it ices."

"I don't—"

"You do." He kicked the screen door open and carried her inside.

"Put me down! I can hop on one foot wherever I need to go."

"Maybe so, but you'll get a free ride this time," he retorted.

She uttered a sound of outrage as he lowered her into a cowhide armchair in the living room. Raitt ignored her indignation, topped a footstool with a sheepskin throw pillow and positioned her ankle on it.

"The ice is this way, I see," he said, passing through a door to the kitchen.

Dunc and Vangie came through the doorway at the opposite end of the living room. "I just love log houses," Vangie was saying. Seeing her in the chair, they stopped, then hurried to her side.

"That bad, gal?" Dunc asked, eyeing the footstool and pillow. "Anything broken?"

"No. Only a sprain."

Vangie was glancing around. "Where is Raitt?"

"Mr. Know-It-All," Jessica snapped, "is in the kitchen, being a busybody."

"Ah," Dunc and Vangie responded in unison. They looked sideways at each other and smiled secretively.

Jessica struggled to get out of the deep chair. Dunc clamped one big hand on her shoulder and pressed her back.

"Gal, you just settle yourself in Raitt's hands, since he knows all the 911 stuff."

"I don't need his emergency aid," Jessica flared. "All I need is a snug riding boot around this ankle and I'll be—"

"Here you go," Raitt interrupted, returning from the kitchen with an ice pack he'd made of a plastic bag and a kitchen towel. He knotted the pack around her ankle before she could flounder up from the chair.

"I'm not going to sit here and—"

Raitt held up a hand. "You won't get your foot in a boot for a week if you don't sit still and let the ice keep the swelling down."

"Vangie, come see your room," said Dunc, hastily taking his guest's arm and leading her to the bedroom wing.

Raitt raked a hand through his hair and gave Jessica a resolute look. "I'll get the suitcases out of the car."

Crossing her arms over her chest, Jessica scowled and watched him shoulder through the screen door. She resented the way he'd taken charge, hauled her inside like a sack of horse feed, and begun issuing high-handed orders right and left. It seemed to have escaped him that he was an unwelcome visitor here, that she was an unwilling hostess.

If Vangie was anything like her grandson, she wouldn't be welcome for long at Patton Ranch, either. No, ma'am. No one ever ordered or pushed Dunc Patton around. Jessica stuck out her chin and vowed to show Raitt Marlow that no one delivered ultimatums to Dunc's granddaughter, either.

She tried to rotate her ankle and disprove Raitt's diagnosis. The movement tore a gasp of pain from her.

Raitt walked in the door just then. He paused, gripping a suitcase in each hand. "Where to with these?"

Too incensed to speak, she pointed down the hall.

"Just grin and bear it, Jess," Raitt recommended wryly. "That's what I intend to do until my grandmother sees the light and stops this foolishness."

He headed down the hall toward the bedroom wing. On the way, he took note of the rustic furnishings and homespun decor. The old log home had a no-frills, frontier charm and a welcoming, wide-open warmth he found hard to resist.

For his grandmother's sake, he wanted to resist it all—the house and the solitary beauty of the remote highland valley.

He saw Vangie pop her head through an open doorway. "Bring mine in here, Raitt," she called. "Your room is around the corner. Isn't this just lovely?"

"Right grand scenery from the window here," Dunc pointed out, pushing aside the red calico curtains to maximize a stunning view of the Warner mountains.

Feeling a small measure of relief, Raitt saw that Vangie would be sleeping in a single bed. Not a lot of room for two people there. Still, he didn't trust that Dunc's intentions were sterling. Men would always be men. It took one to know one.

Dunc chuckled, following Raitt's gaze. "I picked the flower bouquets myself, but Jessie arranged 'em to look nice. She sewed up these curtains and hand-stitched the calico bedspread, too, some years ago. Not a bad cook, either, that gal. Which reminds me, I'd better see to my own cookin', while y'all get settled 'n freshened."

"We'll only be a few minutes," Vangie said, admiringly watching him leave her bedroom. When he could be heard whistling down the hall, she turned to Raitt. "A fine man, isn't he? Didn't I tell you there was little for you to worry about where Dunc Patton is concerned?"

Raitt laid her suitcase on the bed. "You did fail to mention that his granddaughter is thirty-something and single."

"Now, Raitt. What does it matter, since you and she are incidental to my visit here with Dunc? Either way, you would have insisted on coming here as my most protective male relative."

"I'm opposed to being even incidentally set up." Raitt gave Vangie a reproachful frown. "Jess feels the same and flatly told me so. If she objects, as I do, to grandparents advertising in the Personals, she and I have a lot in common."

Vangie cheerily waved off his remarks and bent to smell the wildflowers on the oval-mirrored dressing table. "It's a welcome coincidence," she said, "if you consider that you're both single and love horses. That gives you even more in common with each other."

"I'm not looking for common ground with Jessica Marlow," Raitt objected. "I have a full, satisfying life in San Francisco."

"Raitt, you live alone, rarely date, spend all of your spare time helping street kids. Your life is commendable, but not as full and satisfying as I know it can be. If you'd overlook the divorces in our family, you'd see what I mean."

"Overlook them?" Raitt was incredulous. "You and I are the only undivorced members of the family. Splitting up is a family tradition."

Vangie leveled her gaze at Raitt. "From the first day to the last, my own marriage was blissfully happy, Raitt."

"Yours was the only happy one." Raitt plunged his hands into his pockets. He didn't add that in his opinion, her happy marriage had been a fluke. He loved her too much to hurt her.

"Raitt, divorce isn't a fatal virus, yet you insist on believing you'll be fatally infected if you marry."

"I'll stay single and immune, thank you. Never married, never divorced, I always say."

"Nonsense. It's high time you changed your tune." She buried her nose in the mass of blooms. "There are bouquets of these in your room, too, around the hall and to the left. The door with the horseshoe latch."

Knowing she'd only refute anything else he had to say against marriage, Raitt withdrew and followed her directions. His room was much like hers, decorated in blue calico instead of red. The narrow bed must be the twin to Vangie's, he observed, already feeling acute discomfort. She was lucky to be five foot three instead of six foot two.

He set down his suitcase and checked out the bathroom. The second door that led into it—and the chenille bathrobe hanging on the back of the door—told him he'd be sharing with Dunc's granddaughter. Additional evidence was the container of bath salts by the claw-footed bathtub and a tiny sample vial of gardenia perfume on the pine shelf above the sink.

The sample was too small and too full for him to discount Jessica's claim that she never wore fragrance—or dresses or sheer stockings or pumps.

What man could ignore that she wore her fierce, prickly independence like a bulletproof vest?

Raitt rolled his eyes at himself in the mirror. He had anticipated meeting an adolescent tomboy, not a mature, complex woman. Not a modern spinster. There was nothing old-maidish about her perfume, though. He yielded to a purely male impulse and lifted the vial to his nose.

The scent refreshed his memory of the physical and sexual awareness he had experienced when he'd broken her fall . . . her breasts pressed against him . . . the agile strength of her arms and legs.

Her hair had felt sleek and silky when it had brushed his cheek. Her eyes had darkened from sage green to a deep, passionate emerald, reflecting her fury, embarrassment, pain. Later, he'd caught them examining him with wary interest.

He felt flattered and strangely attracted to her. She had strength of character. Conviction. He couldn't say he didn't value such qualities in a woman. They were just as tempting and arousing as her erotic perfume. Though he was immune to marriage, he wasn't immune to enjoying sex or romance or just plain admiring a woman.

He murmured her name under his breath. "Jess." The single syllable had a sexy, sibilant sound he liked a lot—but not enough to inspire any deep affection. He had limits for how far he'd allow his feelings to go and he never crossed the line.

He returned Jess's perfume to the shelf, reluctant to part with the scent. Setting it back in its place next to a solitary lipstick tube, he recalled how Jess's lips had matched her shell-pink dress. He couldn't deny feeling partial to that delicate color right now.

Partial enough to be thinking of Jess's sprain as sort of fortunate for the man who'd carry her to dinner.

3

JESSICA GLARED AT RAITT as he walked in and halted in front of her chair. Thumbs hooked in his front belt loops, he cocked his head in a silent question regarding how she felt.

He'd changed from chambray and twill into gray, pleat-front slacks and a silky-looking, white shirt. His eyes were a shade of blue she couldn't resist losing herself in for a suspended moment. They brought to mind the deep waters of Morning Glory Lake where Dunc had taught her to fly-fish for rainbow trout.

Jessica suddenly felt wonderstruck, the same feeling she'd had at her first glimpse of the lake. Serene and violet-blue, it lay nestled amid wildflowers and blooming vines in a high mountain meadow. Her mind had grown numb, her heart had leaped, her soul had stirred.

From far away, it seemed, Raitt was asking, "Where's everyone else?"

He stepped close, bent forward, placed his hands flat on the overstuffed arms of her chair.

"They're..." Jessica drew back and took in a steadying breath. "...up in the attic. Digging out an old pair of crutches stored up there."

"Crutches," Raitt repeated, as if he found the word mildly offensive.

"Granddad fractured his leg once thirty years ago, and needed them," she explained, focusing straight ahead to avoid Raitt's eyes. "He was saddle-breaking a stallion and got bucked off."

Raitt's collar was unbuttoned and she found herself staring at the crisp, golden chest hair that filled the opening above the second button. How far down his broad chest did the golden pattern extend?

Shocked by the thought, she squeezed her eyes shut. Through the ceiling she could hear the muffled sounds of Dunc and Vangie in the attic. Close by, she felt warmth emanating from Raitt's body. It spurred desire within her, unwanted desire, enough to refuel her chagrin.

"I don't need you hovering over me," she told him, her tone sharp and short. "I'm not a swooner with a case of the vapors."

Looking both annoyed and disappointed, he straightened and rehooked his thumbs into his belt loops. "How are you feeling otherwise?"

"As soon as I'm up on the crutches, I'll feel divine."

Dunc and Vangie came in, brushing dust from their hands. "Can't find 'em," Dunc announced. "I must have sawed 'em up for kindlin' or something. Raitt, you don't mind bein' my grandgal's helper-outer again, do you?"

Jessica saw one corner of Raitt's mouth quirk up, the other quirk down. He obviously wasn't making a big effort to appear enthusiastic about being her personal porter.

"At your service, Jess," he said.

"Granddad, those crutches have got to be up there. I saw them last month. They— Granddad, come back here."

Dunc was backtracking to the kitchen with Vangie. "Dinner's 'bout ready on the rear deck," he said over his shoulder. "Hop to, you two."

"Great idea," Jess decided. She pulled herself out of the chair and balanced on one foot, ready to hop.

Raitt clasped his hand around her wrist. "Stop acting so put-upon. Is letting me carry you from here to the table that much of a threat to your true grit?"

"It's an even greater indignity, Raitt. Step out of my way, please, and pretend you aren't here."

He blocked her way. "Hopping isn't good for your sprain. There's nothing for you to hold on to between here and the kitchen. A fall will complicate your injury."

You're complicating everything else! she wanted to shout. Less than an hour had passed since Raitt Marlow's arrival, but everything had gone awry. She'd be sharing her bathroom with a hunk instead of the sedate matron she'd expected. He'd sing in the shower, steam up the mirror, be a constant distraction...a fulltime attraction.

The minute she got Granddad all alone, she'd scourge him for withholding vital, crucial information!

She could hear Dunc and Vangie rattling pans in the kitchen. Gritting her teeth, she took an experimental hop on her good foot.

Raitt didn't permit another. He stepped in and swept her off her feet as he had done earlier.

She struggled, but his hold on her was unyielding. "Damn you, Raitt," she gasped.

"Quiet down," he commanded, standing still and steady as he cradled her in his arms. "I'm bigger and stronger than you are. Face facts and quit fighting me."

"Raitt, I won't be treated like a helpless, ditzy damsel in distress. I'll never allow a brute like you to—"

He cut her off with a hot, husky whisper into her ear. "Not a brute. Just a man. Have you been without so long that you've forgotten what a big help one can be?"

Jessica felt the heat of his breath, his lips moving against her hair, his heart beating under the open hand she braced against his chest. She breathed in his scent, a sporty note of lime with a manly undertone of musk.

"I don't need any man's help," she retorted, but the denial came out sounding choppy, unconvincing. Raitt's hold was too firm for her to breathe with ease. His lips were making heated, heady contact with her earlobe.

He moved them, whispered, "Everyone needs a helping hand now and then. Even you, Jess."

"I don't—"

"Right now you do," he murmured against the side of her throat. "Don't kick and scratch anymore. It won't do you a bit of good. All right?"

Jessica wasn't sure if his nodding was making her do the same, or if she'd begun agreeing of her own accord. Nor did she seem to be in control of her arms when they surrendered to Raitt's seductive coaxing and draped themselves loosely around his neck.

Only in her dreams had she been held and nuzzled like this. Only then had she felt dizzy and utterly female, unresisting and irresistible, as Raitt was making her feel right now.

How was he doing it? Making her feel weightless and boneless? Making her wilt against him and accept his male strength and power? It was beyond her.

"Come and get it," Dunc called from outside.

"Hungry, Jess?" Raitt inquired, his breath soft and warm in her ear again.

He knew what he was doing, yet he couldn't control a powerful urge to gentle her. Maybe he'd been without female companionship too long, he reflected hazily. Or maybe it was just . . . No, he had to face it. It was Jess making him feel sexy and seductive. If she was the only provocation, was that really so great a surprise?

No, he decided, as he nipped the edge of her earlobe. Sex was always the core of male-female attraction. Her stubborn, feisty spirit challenged him to wrestle with it. It was as simple as that. It was equally arousing to discover that Jess could be gentled.

But not for long.

Red-faced, she renewed her struggle. For the second time she sputtered, "Brute." Again, he held her in an unyielding embrace.

"Stop it, Raitt," she demanded. "You'll never sweet-talk me!"

Her uneven tone made him feel certain that she could be quieted again, if he put his mind to it. Jess was too much of a challenge to resist. He'd gentle her again, soon.

Vangie and Dunc were already seated on one side of the picnic table when he carried Jess out a moment later. They were toasting each other with wine, oblivious of having dinner companions.

Seated at Raitt's side across from Dunc, Jessica saw her grandfather gaze into Vangie's eyes over the rim of his wineglass. He looked shamelessly besotted, unconscious of everything else. Vangie looked the same.

Jessica had to clear her throat twice to get their attention. "May we join in the toast, Granddad?"

"Why, sure," Dunc replied and poured them both glasses. "We've toasted the *Ranch Roundup* classifieds twice so far."

Reserving her personal opinion of those classifieds, Jessica joined in a four-way clinking of glasses. She hoped that drinking enough red wine would dull her awareness of Raitt. He was sharpening it by sitting too close for comfort on the redwood bench. Or maybe this was just a hotter summer evening than usual.

The last light of the sunset was casting a golden glow across the clear sky. Golden. Like Raitt's hair. She vowed not to look his way again.

As Dunc filled four plates with juicy ribs and hearty chili, Vangie began telling about how she'd grown up on a Texas cattle ranch. Jessica listened with a growing sense of guilt and disloyalty toward her own grandmother. Would Lizbeth want Dunc to be making eyes at another woman?

Deciding that Dunc was too infatuated and Vangie too congenial and likable, Jessica pounced on the only noticeable inconsistency she'd been able to detect so far.

"You don't talk like a Texan, ma'am," she observed.

Vangie grinned. Sounding just like Dunc, she drawled, "Jessie-gal, I broke that habit on purpose, to keep Frisco folks from treatin' me like a bimbo hick. Talkin' like they talk is lots easier than changin' their minds." She dropped the accent. "I lapse occasionally, but not very often."

"Only when you cuss," Raitt put in, smiling.

"Doesn't everyone?" Vangie retorted sweetly.

"Sure do hope so," said Dunc. "I'd hate for Jessie and me to be the only ones colorin' up our language around here."

Once again, he and Vangie looked at each other as if they were beholding heaven on earth.

Jessica drank more wine to bolster her disbelief in love at first sight. The idea was as simple-minded and farfetched as Dunc's stubborn insistence that her own prince would come. Raitt didn't fill that bill. Being a royal pain was the closest he had come so far.

"Raitt," Vangie went on, "tell Dunc and Jessie about the good deeds you do on the streets of San Francisco."

Raitt declined, shaking his head. "I'd rather hear someone else's story."

Jessica felt him looking sideways at her. His elbow nudged hers, a broader hint. She reached for her wine but the glass was empty.

Raitt wouldn't be deterred. "Have you always lived here on the ranch, Jess?"

"No."

"She practically did," Dunc filled in obligingly. "Spent every summer and school holiday out here with Lizbeth and me after her dad—my son, Don—and her mom moved south to Los Angeles. Don and Beth never liked ranch life, either one, but Jessie-gal took to it as soon as she could crawl. Lizbeth and I raised her 'bout as much as her own folks did."

"Well, well," Vangie remarked, looking supremely pleased. "Raitt and his brother spent several boyhood summers at my sister's ranch in Texas."

"Don't forget why we summered there," Raitt said, his expression sour.

"Their parents' bitter divorce and custody battles were part of the reason," Vangie explained. "Certain people should never be married to each other, but try telling them that before they embark on marriage. They had to live and learn."

Raitt raised an eyebrow. "Like everyone else in the family, except you and Grandpa Leland—and me."

"This is neither the time nor the place, Raitt." Vangie looked at Jessica. "As I was saying, he learned to ride and rope at the ranch. No one was surprised when he became a mounted patrol officer—one of the best, I might add."

"Any brothers and sisters, Jess?" Raitt inquired, discomfited by his grandmother's curt rebuke and her shameless sales pitch.

Jessica nodded. "A married sister, Robyn. She's like Mom and Dad in preferring L.A. to here."

That was all Jess cared to offer; this forced exchange of information was all for nothing. Nor was there any point in mentioning that every married member of the Patton family was, or had been, happily hitched. Raitt's few, bitter words had communicated a bleak view of love and marriage. If he wasn't a marrying man, this setup was doubly useless.

"Don't know what I'd have done without this gal, these past many years," said Dunc. "Best ranch hand I ever had. Knows horses, cattle and—"

"No better teacher than Granddad," she cut in.

Raitt must be wishing he'd never set foot on the ranch. Recalling the moment he'd stepped out of his car, she wondered what he must have thought when he got his first good look at her. The faces of her three mail-order suitors had fallen at first glance. Thanks to the sunset and the dust today, she had been spared another blow.

Looking at the sky, and beyond the deck to the mountains, Raitt said, "It's more beautiful here than I imagined. Quite a surprise."

"Reminds me of parts of Wyoming and Montana," Dunc said. "The Durango area of Colorado, too."

"It's just perfect," Vangie added. "Aren't you glad we made the trip, Raitt?"

"It's a nice break from city life," he allowed. He swirled the wine in his glass, then glanced at Jess. "There must be some pretty decent riding trails around here."

"Miles and miles of 'em," Dunc piped up when Jessica failed to respond. "Prettiest views you've ever seen from the highest lookouts. If you like to fly-fish, Raitt, Jessie can take you up to Mornin' Glory Lake. It's too far on horseback for me at my age or I'd ride along. You can use my fly rod."

"Thanks, Dunc, but who's going to chaperon the elders if Jess and I go fishing?"

"Trust me, boy, I'm a gentleman through 'n through. Ask any of the ranchers round here and they'll tell you the same. Dunc Patton's word is solid as a rock. Come to think of it, can you guarantee you'll treat Jessie with the same measure of respect?"

"Granddad . . ." Jessica put a strong warning in her tone. "I'm not a potted plant. I *am* present at this table and quite capable of speaking for myself."

Dunc looked only slightly chastened. "'Course you are. Don't know what devil got into me."

"I guarantee it, Dunc." Raitt put out his hand and exchanged a firm handshake with Dunc.

Looking around, Jessica saw that only she was appalled by the smug, male-chauvinist agreement the two men had just struck. It made her doubly determined to pull Granddad aside as soon as possible and give him a tongue-lashing. He was acting positively medieval.

As for Raitt, his involvement in Dunc's archaic bargain was galling. It went a giant step beyond the deference a proper guest owed his host.

"Unfortunately, I'll be too busy to go fishing with anyone," she said to the table at large. "This is my week to sink new fence posts at the end of the valley. The old ones are rotting at ground level."

Dunc shrugged. "It's nothin' that can't wait a week or two. A day of fishin'll do you good, gal. You know you love to fish."

Jessica was searching her mind for bigger, better excuses when Raitt spoke up. "Jess's ankle probably won't be well enough for riding and fishing for a day or two."

She felt a rush of gratitude to Raitt for bailing her out, yet felt dense for not coming up with that obvious excuse herself.

Then she realized that Raitt had conveniently bailed *himself* out.

She'd been politely rejected. The sting was sharper than if he'd inflicted it rudely and thoughtlessly.

By the end of a day or two, Vangie and Dunc might decide against each other, she told herself in an effort to soothe the sting. Raitt would leave with Vangie, and all would be well again.

It was growing dark outside, so Dunc lighted two candle lamps. Raitt helped clear the table after dinner and returned from the kitchen with a fresh ice pack.

Still smarting inwardly, Jessica reversed her position on the bench and submitted without argument when he knelt to remove the first, half-melted pack.

"How does it feel, Jess? Painful?"

"No. The ice makes it numb." Numb enough for her to hardly feel his touch, especially if she kept her attention on the stars.

Through the open kitchen window, she could hear Dunc and Vangie rinsing dinner plates and talking in low tones. She remembered how openly affectionate he and Lizbeth had been with each other, how generous with kisses and hugs. How long before he'd betray Lizbeth and kiss Vangie? Any minute now, from the sound of things.

How could he?

"I hate to think what my grandfather would say if he could see his widow making eyes at another man," Raitt said. "Would your grandmother say the same if she could see Dunc right now?"

Jessica nodded. "She'd want him to be happy, but not foolishly so, I'm sure. He and Vangie are acting like adolescents, if you ask me."

"They're not displaying a shred of caution. I don't like it."

"I agree." Jessica had lowered her gaze and now it was caught by the rich, flickering glow of candlelight on Raitt's bent head. How would his hair feel if she furrowed her fingers through it? How many women had done so and satisfied their own burning curiosity?

She switched back to stargazing. Too much red wine, she told herself. Too much Raitt Marlow, as well. His palm was cupped around her instep, warming the sole of her foot. Where she really should be feeling some pain, she was feeling only pleasure, thinking only of Cinderella—and of the prince, fitting Cinderella's foot into the glass slipper.

"Almost no swelling," Raitt murmured. "Good." He paused, glancing at the kitchen window. "It's awfully quiet in there, all of a sudden."

"Too quiet," Jessica agreed.

"What do you suppose they're doing?"

"God only knows."

"Maybe one of them went to the bathroom."

"Maybe." She thought of her own bathroom; Raitt would be showering and shaving and brushing his teeth there. Looking down again, she found him staring back, as if he'd forgotten all about Dunc and Vangie.

"You have the slimmest ankles, Jess."

She felt him slowly encircle her ankle with his thumb and forefinger, measuring the joint. His palm still cupped her instep.

"You...simply have...have long fingers." *And the bluest eyes, the broadest shoulders, the richest golden hair.*

"Can't take a compliment at face value, Jess?" he mocked gently. "Why not?"

"Hey, out there," Dunc called through the window. "Vangie and I are goin' for a little evenin' stroll down the driveway. Not far. We'll take Murph and Muttley along. How's that ankle, Raitt?"

"First-class," Raitt replied. "Don't do anything a good Boy Scout wouldn't do during your stroll. Don't forget what we shook on, either."

Dunc gave them a jaunty farewell wave. "Solid as a rock, boy."

"He'd better be," Raitt muttered, turning back to Jess.

He looked at his fingers braceleted around her ankle. *First-class. No lie.* Her skin was smooth and warm. Her pretty pink toes curled into the cradle of his palm. He found himself wanting to slip his hand higher and palm the shape of her calf, her knee, her thigh.

But she hadn't accepted his sincere compliment, so what made him imagine she'd accept an exploratory caress? For that matter, would he want his grandmother to accept similar explorations from Dunc tonight? No!

He quickly wrapped the fresh ice pack around Jess's sprain and secured it with the towel.

"Thank you," she said, sounding relieved. "Would you mind doing me a favor?"

"Not at all." His mind began conjuring up more than one favor he'd like to do. "What?"

"Double-check the attic for those crutches."

The last thing on his mind, he thought ruefully. "How do I get up there?"

"In the laundry room, next to the kitchen, there's a pull-down ladder from the ceiling. The attic light automatically switches on when you pull the ladder down."

"Jess, I don't mind carrying you."

"*I* mind, Raitt."

"Yeah." He stood. "You make that more than clear." Her chin was jutting out again, her lips were tight and tense. She looked as if she needed a long, wet kiss a lot more than she needed crutches.

He turned on his heel before he could act on the impulse.

Once inside the laundry room, he pulled down the overhead ladder. The automatic light came on. He climbed the ladder until his head rose above the attic floor level. The space was full of dusty odds and ends, shadeless lamps, rickety chairs, an enormous cedar chest. Leaning against the chest, in plain view, were two wooden crutches.

Raitt shook his head at the pitiful lengths two optimistic grandparents would go to, just to match up their single grandchildren.

Outside on the deck, Jessica watched a shooting star in the night sky. A beautiful night for a romantic walk, but she had no doubt that Dunc and Vangie only had eyes for each other. They were probably kissing out there like teenagers. She imagined herself kissing Raitt, and an entirely adult jolt of heat and desire shot through her.

She hoped he'd find those crutches. He was evidently making a lengthier search than Dunc and Vangie had—if they had searched at all. She had suspected all along that they'd fibbed about the crutches, just to force her and Raitt together.

Raitt had been gone quite a while. Or did it just seem so long because she was alone at the table? Maybe. He made time fly when he was present. On the other hand, he'd already been at the ranch far too long. Damn him. He'd skewed everything, even time.

Her heartbeat quickened when she heard the kitchen door open behind her.

"Not a crutch to be seen," Raitt said, sliding next to her on the bench.

"Oh." Hard to believe Dunc and Vangie hadn't conspired, but here was proof. "Thank you for taking the trouble to look."

"No trouble." That wasn't quite true; it troubled him that he hadn't been thinking rationally up there. He'd thought only of carrying Jess to bed later tonight, of the rousing battle she'd wage—and lose—all the way to her bedroom.

But then, feeling a rush of attraction as he glanced into Jess's starlit eyes, he wondered if he should have reached for those crutches the way a drowning sailor reaches for a lifeline.

4

UNFAMILIAR SOUNDS woke Jessica the next morning. Water splashing. Someone whistling a jaunty tune. Raitt Marlowe in the shower.

She groaned into her pillow, still incensed. Raitt had carried her to her bedroom last night and practically tucked her into bed despite her loud objections. Now he was using up all the hot water. But even her chagrin could not repress a steamy image of him soaping his body under the hot spray—nude, wet, muscular, male.

Rejecting that stimulating image took more effort than Jessica felt should be necessary. She tried to concentrate on other things. The tune he was whistling suggested he'd slept well last night. Scowling, she covered her head with her pillow. She hadn't slept well and wasn't waking refreshed.

Her sprained ankle was throbbing painfully, as it had all night. And the rest of her body continued to manifest a ridiculous attraction to the man who had caused the sprain. Desire was engulfing her.

She clutched the pillow tighter against her ears. She hadn't been assailed by desire since...since Budd. Abrupt and self-absorbed, he hadn't proven to be the most pleasing lover. Since then she had experienced her own satisfaction in private, not in the arms of a man. And *never* in a shower with a hunk like Raitt....

She cut that thought short, threw aside the pillow, and heard Raitt turn off the water. The image of him toweling himself dry mushroomed in her mind. She imagined the friction of the towel on his hard chest, his firm stomach, his—

From now on, she vowed, *I wake and shower first.*

She stoically endured the sound of him turning the basin tap on and off as he shaved. Then the other bathroom door closed and her thoughts were her own again.

TEETH GRITTED against the sharp, splintering pain, Jessica hopped on one foot to the kitchen some twenty minutes later. Making no concessions to houseguests this morning, she had slicked her wet hair into a ponytail and dressed as usual in worn jeans and a faded plaid workshirt. Her sprained foot was still too swollen to fit into a riding boot, so she wore a moccasin instead.

Murph and Muttley snoozed under the table, while Dunc and Raitt drank coffee at the table. Raitt wore Levi's and his blue chambray shirt. Vangie, dressed too much like a hoedown square dancer for Jessica's taste, was presiding over the kitchen stove. *As if she's already married to Granddad,* Jessica thought.

"Mornin', gal," Dunc said with a wide smile. "Sleep okay?"

"No." As soon as these intruders went back home she'd sleep okay, but not until then. She saw that Vangie had fixed a small vase of wildflowers for the breakfast table. What was she taking out of the oven? Biscuits. What simmered on the top burner? Pan gravy. Dunc's all-time favorite breakfast.

"You shouldn't be up on your ankle like that," Raitt said, frowning. "Sit down and elevate it."

Jessica ignored the unsolicited advice and lurched toward the coffee maker.

Vangie stepped into her path and made amiable, shooing motions. "Please sit and rest your sprain, Jessie. I'll see to dishing up breakfast and serving everybody. How do you take your coffee?"

"Blacker than sin," Jessica replied. She felt like adding darkly that this kitchen was her own and Lizbeth's, not Vangie's. It wasn't Vangie's place to rustle up breakfast, or to make things more cheerful and homey than they'd been since Lizbeth's death.

Smiling, Vangie poured coffee into a cup. "Raitt, give Jessie a helping hand to the table, please."

"I don't need a hand, Mrs. Marlow." Jessica managed a short shuffle toward the table and tried not to grimace with pain.

Raitt rose, took three giant steps across the kitchen and scooped her into his arms. "You need a strong dose of common sense, Jess."

"Darn right she does," Dunc agreed.

Jessica endured the brief, forced transfer to the table in tight-lipped silence. Clasped too close against

Raitt's body, smelling the fresh scents of castile soap and lime shaving foam, she knew she'd find it hard to speak, anyway. A cold shower had cooled her off, but being in Raitt's relentless grip was making her flush all over again.

His hair was still damp, a golden lock springing over his forehead, making her think of palomino stallions. She had to catch her breath after he set her down in the chair next to his.

"Granddad," she said as soon as she could speak, "that pair of crutches is *somewhere* in the attic. I know you looked last night, and so did Raitt, but—"

"He did?" Dunc gulped.

Raitt met the older man's uncertain gaze. "Nowhere to be seen."

"Would you look just one more time, Granddad?"

Dunc raised his bristly eyebrows at Raitt. "Care to help me search around?"

"Sure."

Raitt followed him out of the kitchen. Once in the attic, Dunc leaned against a rafter and broke into a sheepish grin. He gestured at the crutches.

"Why'd you leave 'em there, Raitt?"

"Out of respect for my grandmother and my host, I guess."

"Couldn't be that you like my Jessie-gal more than you expected?"

Raitt shrugged. "If Vangie didn't tell you I'm not a marrying man, she should have."

"She told me over the phone. Just like I told her Jessie's too hotheaded, proud and stubborn to be anybody's obedient wife. She's been dead set against partnerin' up, ever since one of my cowpunks broke her heart 'way back."

Raitt rolled his eyes. "So why are our grandparents trying to fix the two of us up with each other?"

"Hope springs eternal, boy. You can't deny you and my grand-gal have a lot in common—both love horses and shy away from entanglements, both hotheaded, both proud 'n' stubborn."

"I have a healthy interest in the female sex," Raitt said, "but none in getting involved."

"Well, if you romance Jessie-gal a little, I'm not goin' to punch your lights out, Raitt. But you break her heart with empty expectations and I'll break your cover-boy face."

"I'll do the same to yours if you hurt Vangie, Dunc, no disrespect intended."

Dunc looked wounded. "I'm a marryin' man, boy. My expectations lead straight to 'I do.'"

"Mine don't."

"I've got that straight," Dunc assured him. He paused, looking thoughtful. "Just for your information, I've lived long enough to've learned a little bit about how women think, no matter who they are. Take Lizbeth, for instance. She could be as stubborn as Jessie, but all I had to do to loosen her up was call her Miss Lizbeth at the right moment and she'd melt like ice cream in July."

"I'll keep that in mind, Dunc."

"Now carry them crutches down to Jessie before she hippety-hops herself into worse shape than she's in."

They shook hands on their man-to-man understanding, then Raitt followed Dunc down the ladder with the crutches.

"Hallelujah!" Jessica whooped when she saw them. Her joy lessened the guilty funk that had settled over her during Raitt and Dunc's absence.

She'd drunk Vangie's black-as-sin coffee and enjoyed it more than the dark brew Lizbeth used to make. She had taste-tested some biscuit with gravy and found it mouth-meltingly better than Lizbeth's recipe. Every favorable reaction to Vangie's cooking made her feel disloyal and traitorous to Lizbeth's memory.

The crutches were a welcome sight. Raitt held them out, and she took them with a sigh of relief. She also felt a secret measure of regret that she wouldn't be experiencing Raitt up close, personally, after this.

She felt piqued when he looked immensely relieved to be rid of the chore.

Up on the crutches, she moved to the kitchen door with little trouble. "I'll see to the horses," she said. "Come, Murph. Come, Muttley."

The two dogs bounded outside through the dog-door.

"You've barely eaten a bite," Vangie protested.

"This is a working ranch. I have work to do, animals to be fed and watered."

"Gal, we got guests here to entertain, and that sprain you've got won't get well in the stable."

Immune to their arguments, she pushed open the screen door and crossed the backyard to the stable. The morning air was brisk, and birds twittered in the pines. The stable smelled comfortingly of hay, horses and straw.

She whistled to the horses to come in from their paddocks to their stalls for feed and water. They'd been trained that way for her to keep tabs on each one's intake.

Her wild black stallion, Alamo, nickered as she approached his stall. An egomaniac, he had to be greeted first or peace wouldn't reign.

"Good morning, you big, selfish, sexy stud."

She knew that his inflated opinion of himself had nothing to do with her lavish praise, and everything to do with Teardrop and Aunt Lucille, the two mares at the far end of the stable. Both seemed to agree with him that he was the studliest four-legged male on the ranch. Marcus and Speed, on the other hand, were middle-aged geldings who never overstepped their neutral status in the equine social order. Young, uncut and unbroken, Alamo was king.

He was fresh and feisty today, nipping at her fingers, sniffing her shirt pocket, while the two chestnut geldings were genial and complacent as she greeted them. Like Aunt Lucille, they were old enough to have seen it all.

Teardrop whinnied softly and rubbed her velvety nose into Jessica's cupped palm. She traced the tear-shaped white spot on the shy, young mare's forehead.

"How does your little one grow?" she murmured. Teardrop was pregnant with Alamo's seed.

Jessica had watched their mating ritual with unabashed awe. Breeding was a routine ritual on a cattle ranch, nothing to cause a rancher to blush. She had witnessed countless such unions between bulls and cows, stallions and mares, roosters and hens. Her night with Budd hadn't been remarkably different, she reflected. Males always came out on top.

The thought of Raitt Marlow in that position made her blush and hide her hot face in Teardrop's glossy mane. The mare's stomach rumbled, reminding Jessica that the animals needed their breakfast.

She turned to the task of feeding and watering, and immediately realized she couldn't handle either a water pail or a pitchfork today, with or without crutches. She remembered Dunc cursing the same fate when he'd broken his leg long ago. Until now she hadn't fully appreciated his impairment.

"Need a hand with anything?" Raitt inquired behind her.

Startled, she pivoted around. "I can manage as soon as I grow a third arm."

"Admit the obvious, Jess. You're stumped. Tell me what to do and I'll do it."

Jessica could see from his determined stance that an argument wouldn't stop him from helping out. If she didn't tell this horse cop what to do, he'd do it all his own way.

"Two flakes of hay for each horse, Alamo first. Five-gallon bucket of water. Be careful of Alamo. He's a wild one."

Raitt took the pitchfork. "Dunc already warned me. He says you bought Alamo and Teardrop at a wild-horse auction. Interesting."

From Jessica's point of view, standing behind him, nothing was half as interesting as the way his shirt molded against his broad shoulders every time he separated a flake from the bale with the hayfork. He looked strong enough to flake hay all day without breaking into a sweat.

He glanced over his shoulder and caught her with her mouth open. She snapped it shut and switched her attention to Alamo. His ears were pricked forward at Raitt. He seemed to be measuring Raitt's manliness, too.

"There's not enough open range land left for wild horse herds to roam," she said. "Beyond that, they're vulnerable to disease, drought, natural predators. I went to the auction just to look and fell in love instead. These two were all I could afford."

Raitt paused, leaning on the fork handle. "Dunc says they'd probably have ended up in the glue factory if you hadn't had a soft heart for them."

"Sensible rather than soft," she corrected curtly. Only Dunc had the right to know how soft a touch she could be. After Budd and his bet, she'd never be soft in the heart again.

"Nothing wrong with having a tender spot for a good cause," Raitt said reproachfully. "I've got my own good cause—street kids. Like wild horses, homeless kids are struggling to survive, too, against crushing odds. So many come from broken homes."

Jessica recalled his negative remarks about his parents' divorce wars and custody battles and waited for him to add a personal word about his own broken home.

"Two hundred thousand street kids in this country," he went on. "That's a conservative estimate. They're not even counted in the population of the homeless."

"How much are you able to help, Raitt?"

"Never enough. I know how those kids feel. Their parents split up and don't stop fighting, even after the divorce. The kid figures he's at fault, somehow. No one's paying attention to him, he falls in with the wrong crowd..." He shook his head.

"Your parents' divorce hit you hard," she said.

"Yeah." His tone was bitter. "So did my aunt's, uncle's, sister's and brother's. Anything you want to know about the death of love, and life after divorce, I can tell you."

Jessica's heart went out to him. Her own family had fared so well. Dunc and Lizbeth's three children were happy with their mates. Jessica's sister, Robyn, had married at seventeen and beaten the odds against teen marriage. Dunc and Lizbeth had lasted until death parted them.

Jessica had always dreamed of enjoying the same happiness herself—her prince would come, court her, marry her, live happily ever after with her on the ranch. But she just hadn't been born with a face and body that could attract the prince of her dreams. She had "attracted" Budd, the toad, instead.

"In short, you aren't a romantic at heart," she summed up.

He cocked his head. "I have my moments, but they don't lead to the altar. My grandparents' happy marriage was an exception to the family rule, so I don't hold any hope of repeating their success. It was a fluke."

Indignant at being ignored, Alamo snorted, swished his tail and began tap-dancing his front hooves on the stable floor.

"Are your two good causes saddle broken?" Raitt asked, changing the subject.

"Only Teardrop."

"Who tamed her?"

"I did."

Raitt let out a low whistle. "Congratulations."

Feeling a tinge of pink creep into her cheeks, Jessica propelled herself to the end of the stable and scratched Teardrop's white spot.

Raitt pitched two neat, crisp hay flakes into the stallion's manger. "Who's going to break Alamo?"

"Granddad is the true breaker around here. He was a professional for years. No one in the northern half of the state can top him, even now."

"At Dunc's age, breaking Alamo could be suicide," Raitt observed, giving the two geldings and Aunt Lucille their own ration.

Jessica fixed him with a haughty stare, then snapped, "Seventy isn't old."

Her sharp reproach stopped Raitt from retorting that only a fool would break a wild stallion at that advanced age. He bit back the words, seeing how deeply Jess loved Dunc Patton, how much she idolized him, how fiercely loyal she would be to him forever. She even seemed ready to deny that Dunc was mortal and would die someday.

Approaching Teardrop's stall with the last forkful of hay, Raitt gently pointed out, "No one lives forever."

"I'm not listening."

"You do a lot of that," he retorted, losing patience. "I tell you to keep your ankle elevated and you don't hear a word. Look how it's swelling up, dammit."

Jessica set her jaw. "I'm responsible for myself and my ankle is my own business. No one bosses me or my grandfather around. Not you, not Vangie, not anyone else."

She swung around and headed to Alamo's end of the stable. The moment her back was turned, she heard Teardrop nicker tentatively.

"Easy, beauty," she heard Raitt say. "I have a horse, too." His tone grew smooth and seductive as he made friends with Teardrop. "You'd like my horse, Cody. He's patient with everyone, even rowdy street kids. They'd never trust a cop, but a cop on Cody can be irresistible to almost everyone."

At the other end of the stable, Jessica saw the stallion's eyes roll. He clearly didn't like Raitt smooching up to private property. Jessica didn't like it, either. The tone he was using with Teardrop was too appealing, too attractive, like Raitt's street-kid cause.

Glancing back, Jessica felt a spurt of annoyance. Teardrop was batting her long eyelashes and rubbing her delicate nose on Raitt's bicep. An instant pushover for a handsome face.

Alamo let out a jealous neigh and kicked his stall door. Jessica grasped his forelock and brought his eyes level with hers.

"Hey, big guy," she said soothingly. "He's just a man. Cool down, or I'll have to put your stud chain on you."

As she stroked the stallion's quivering jaw and maintained her low, soothing tone, Alamo relaxed a little. All the same, he shifted his attention over her shoulder when he heard Raitt's footsteps approach.

Raitt halted behind Jessica, and she could feel him watching her, listening.

"Just a man," she murmured again to put Raitt in his place. Twining her fingers into Alamo's ebony mane, she nuzzled her nose against his. "Not a super-stud like you."

"Not?" Raitt questioned in a low, throaty murmur. "You've been around horseflesh too long...Miss Jess."

Miss Jess? Her fantasy cowboy prince always called her that.

Alamo chose that moment to toss his head. The force of his movement pushed Jessica back, against Raitt. She dropped her crutches, and Raitt's arms came around her from behind. One arm slid under her breasts, the other firmly clasped her waist.

She could feel his belt buckle against the small of her back. It felt good. Just right. Raitt swayed back into balance and she swayed with him. His hipbones pressed into her bottom, then she felt his lips skimming the shape of her ear.

"Steady, Miss Jess," he whispered.

A torrent of protests stopped short in her throat. She felt her heart thump-thumping in her chest and knew his arm had to feel every escalating beat. He cupped a hand under her left breast as if to register the thumps—or treasure them. She didn't know which, couldn't think as his mouth moved, soft, warm, moist, down the side of her neck to the curve of her shoulder. He kissed the sensitive spot and her knees weakened.

"Raitt," she gasped.

"What?" Raitt half turned her toward him and looked into her eyes. They were darkening from sage green to emerald. Her face was flushed, her throat arched, her lips parted, lifting to his. Her breast was round and firm in his palm, her nipple budding beneath the pad of his thumb. "What do you want, Jess? A little romance?"

He brushed his lips over hers, and she uttered a breathy sound of reluctant, hesitant invitation. Deepening the kiss, seeking her tongue with his, he circled his thumb over and over her nipple. She wasn't resisting and he wasn't, either.

His Levi's were suddenly too tight, for the best of reasons. It didn't seem to matter that Jess was the prickliest, most unreasonable, unmanageable woman he'd ever kissed. She had him as aroused in one instant as he'd ever been in his adult life. It felt good.

Dunc's pet rooster crowed outside, behind the stable. The sound penetrated Jessica's consciousness, provoked a dawning realization of what she was doing. Kissing Raitt. *French*-kissing Raitt. Letting him feel for himself how much he turned her on!

She broke from the heady contact and pushed away his caressing hand. He didn't release the arm he was holding tight around her waist.

"What now?" he asked, his tone thick with desire.

"If Alamo hadn't pushed me, I'd never have—"

"You weren't beating me down with your crutches," he cut in.

"I didn't get a chance." She squirmed against his confining arm. "Let me go."

"No. You've been on your feet long enough."

"I—"

He lifted her against his chest and deposited her on the hay bale. "Don't you ever admit to a weakness or listen to reason, Jess?"

She had rarely felt weaker than at that moment, but wasn't about to admit it. Now he stood glaring at her, hands on his hips, seemingly unaware that directly at her eye level was the shape of his erection in stone-washed blue denim.

She had to force herself to look upward, at his face. His eyes were a blazing blue, his jaw was clenched.

"You're not in much better shape, yourself," he muttered, the angle of his gaze making it clear that her nipples were just as conspicuous. He picked up her crutches and handed them to her.

"Thank you."

"Don't mention it." He took up the water hose and opened the faucet, then began filling a bucket. "I'll finish out here. Go inside."

Jessica gathered the strength to do as he said. Mounting a show of defiance was beyond her at the moment. She needed to regroup and recoup.

Returning to the house, she decided that Raitt must be missing a city girlfriend pretty badly. Deep-kissing a plain Jane and exploring her half-pint bosom couldn't have stimulated that big a response.

Jessica had no illusions, even though she had felt like Cinderella getting the best kiss of her life.

5

JESSICA DIDN'T EXPECT to stumble upon a love scene when she came in from the stable. She couldn't believe she hadn't made enough noise at the back door for Dunc and Vangie to hear her, but they were right in the middle of the kitchen, kissing.

She had to clear her throat loudly before they pulled apart. Dunc didn't even blush. He even kept one arm around Vangie's shoulders. And she looked not at all embarrassed at being caught.

"Where did you leave my grandson?" she said brightly, her dark eyes twinkling.

"He's finishing up in the stable."

"Crutches workin' out for you, gal?"

"Well enough to get around on my own. What are you two doing besides making whoopee?"

Dunc grinned and squeezed Vangie close to his side. "Gettin' ready for the town picnic." He pointed at two rattan hampers on the table. "Packin' up the baskets for it."

"Oh. That." Jessica had forgotten the annual event was today. She had never looked forward to it much.

"I've been tellin' Vangie about the auction and how it's always the high point of the day."

The auction had never been anything but the lowest point for Jessica. Sexist, too. The women made up the baskets, the men bid money for them, and the highest bidder shared the woman's picnic with her. Jessica always dreaded the moment when the only bidder for her basket was her own grandfather.

She had never wormed her way out of donating a basket because the auction benefited Dunc's pet charity. Not only that, the auction was a cherished local tradition. *Everyone* took part.

"Put Vangie's name on both baskets and leave me here at home," Jessica said eagerly; for the first time she had an excuse! "You and Raitt can each buy one."

Dunc gave her a warning look. "Best foot forward, Jessie. You promised."

"We've got lots of last night's ribs and chili to fill up both baskets," Vangie said enthusiastically. "They're half packed already."

"My sprain is too swollen." An excellent excuse. The best she'd ever had. "It'll swell more if I go."

"You'll do fine with ice packs and crutches, gal."

"Granddad—"

"You promised. If you don't go, nobody else here goes."

Vangie looked crestfallen at that possibility. "Oh, Dunc. I've been looking forward to it so much. Your friends and neighbors will all be there. I do want to meet everyone."

"They all want to meet you, too," Dunc assured her. He pushed out his lower lip in an exaggerated pout and directed it at Jessica.

Uncomfortable in the role of party pooper, she relented. "Oh, all right. I'll go."

Vangie applauded the decision. "What should I wear? Will a sleeveless top and a fiesta skirt be all right? And sandals?"

"Sounds fetchin' to me," Dunc replied with a gleam in his eye.

"I'm wearing what I've got on," Jessica declared.

Dunc put his foot down again. "You do, and I guarantee you nobody'll budge out of this house 'till you look more than half-presentable."

"Oh, Dunc." Vangie's face fell again.

Jessica mentally counted to ten. "Okay. I'll wear my *clean* jeans instead of these."

"Along with that embroidery-flower blouse Lizbeth made for one of your birthdays?" Dunc bargained.

"It needs ironing, Granddad." The peasant-style blouse also had a low, elastic-gathered neckline that she had never thought suited her. "Besides, what difference can it possibly make what I—?"

"Please, Jessie," Vangie entreated. "Surely your grandmother hoped you'd wear her gift in her memory every now and then."

Dunc nodded, adding to the guilt quotient. "She gave you that flower perfume one Christmas with the same idea in mind."

Raitt came in just then, but stopped inside the door when they fell abruptly silent. "Am I interrupting something?"

"Yep," Dunc replied. "A Texas standoff. Texas is winnin'." He pushed his pout to its furthest, most guilt-inspiring extent.

"Excuse me until picnic time," Jessica huffed, stomping off to her room. "I have some ironing to do."

JESSICA DIDN'T REAPPEAR until Dunc thumped on her bedroom door and called to her, "Head 'em up. Move 'em out."

"I'm not a herd of cattle, Granddad," she called back at him.

"Stubborn as a herd of mules," he grouched. "You better be dressed. I'm droppin' in to check you out." He opened the door and peeked in. "Well, now. You look two-thirds decent. Don't act so miserable about it. I didn't insist on you wearin' a dress, now, did I?"

Jessica used her crutch to open the door wide. "Grandma's blouse and perfume are as far as I go."

"Smell like a corsage again," he approved, sniffing the air.

"Granddad, have you ever been knocked cold by a crutch?"

He laughed so hard that she had to crack a forgiving smile. She followed him down the hall, out to the front porch, and saw Raitt and Vangie maneuvering the two baskets into the minuscule trunk of Raitt's red sports car.

"I'm drivin' today," Dunc said proudly. "Can't wait to see everybody's eyes pop out when we wheel up in this hot rod."

Jessica peered into the cubbyhole behind the front seat. "We're all going in this?"

"Yep. All four. You and Raitt in back. Me 'n' Vangie in front."

"But your own car is much—"

"I feel like hot-roddin' instead. Raitt offered me the driver's seat if I wanted it, and hot damn, I do."

Jessica darted a frown at Raitt over the top of the car. He shrugged and shut the trunk, acting as if he hadn't stood a chance against Dunc's adolescent wish to make eyes pop at the picnic.

"There's no room back there for anyone, much less the crutches," she objected, picturing herself scrunched into Raitt's lap.

"They'll stick out the window just fine, gal."

"Raitt and I will go in your car."

"Battery's too low in mine. Get yourself in." Dunc opened the door and tipped the driver's seat forward for her convenience.

Getting situated was an awkward business because of her ankle, and became more difficult when Raitt climbed in from the other side. She had to angle her calves across his thighs, dangerously near the zipper of his pants.

He was wearing his khaki twills from the day before and a pale pink polo shirt. She had never seen a man look so masculine in pink.

His face showed no reaction, neither when her legs crossed his, nor when he had to curve his arm around her shoulders to avoid a muscle cramp.

"This is ridiculous," she muttered.

"Only to us," he said. "Everyone else is having the time of their lives."

Jessica crossed her arms over the front of her flower-embroidered blouse. "They need their heads examined."

Dunc got Vangie and the crutches situated up front, and the red-hot sports car was roaring down the highway a few minutes later.

"Banzai!" Dunc exulted, shifting into fifth gear. He started telling Vangie all about the elemental, volcanic forces that had shaped the Warner Mountains and the hidden valleys in the area.

Jessica could only think of the elemental force behind Raitt's zipper and the chest muscles that kept his knit shirt stretched taut in front. She wondered what he was thinking behind his neutral expression.

"That's a beautiful blouse, Jess."

"It's nice of you to say so." She noted that Dunc's right hand had settled on Vangie's nearest knee. He seemed to have forgotten his former marriage. Out of loyalty to Lizbeth, she informed Raitt loudly, "My grandmother made this beautiful blouse. She stitched every one of the three dozen California poppies on it."

"I'll have to count them sometime," Raitt murmured.

Dunc paid no attention, just kept nattering on about volcanoes and lava rock. She had never seen him drive so fast, way over the fifty-five-mile speed limit. Only one hand on the wheel.

She looked at Raitt. "Do you drive this fast?"

"Sure, if I can get away with it. Otherwise I'd have bought a cruiser like Dunc's." He slid a glance her way and repeated one of his lines from the night before. "Something sure smells nice."

"Granddad made me do it," she muttered. "The blouse, too."

"Oh." Raitt was unable to hide a twinge of disappointment; so he hadn't been the reason she had worn poppies and perfume today. He couldn't really pin down why he wanted to be the reason. He couldn't forget that kiss this morning, either.

The legs angled across his lap were slender and strong. Suddenly, he wished she had worn short shorts or a short skirt. But no, she was wearing ankle-length jeans. Her bad ankle was swollen. He touched it and she jumped.

"We should have brought an ice pack for it," he said, curling his fingers around her injured joint. He'd meant it as a soothing gesture, but couldn't help making it a caress.

Jessica couldn't quite meet his blue eyes or warn him to keep his hand to himself. It seemed to fit naturally around her ankle, warm and comforting—the same hand that had earlier cupped her breast.

Raitt kept it right where it was all the way to town. Jessica never found the right moment to set him straight about where his hand did—and didn't—belong. It would have been awkward, anyway, with Vangie and Dunc there to hear every discouraging word.

EYES POPPED AT THE PICNIC when they drove up in Raitt's car—just as Dunc had anticipated. A curious, admiring crowd gathered around them. Dunc began introducing Vangie and Raitt to everyone.

Jessica left the pair in the crowd and wandered over to watch the annual turtle race. She chatted with people here and there and had to explain each time about her ankle and the crutches. Reluctant to mention either Raitt or her own klutziness, she fudged the details.

A baseball game was in progress, as well as volleyball and table tennis matches. Jessica had always been one of the volleyball kingpins, but not today. The shorthanded team was bemoaning her sprain with her on the sidelines when Raitt walked up with an ice pack.

"Guess what it's time for you to do," he said.

"I'm doing just fine without it." She saw the team looking at Raitt, then at her, and knew what they were wondering. "Raitt Marlow," she said, then introduced her teammates.

He shook hands all around. Jessica could see the women rolling their eyes at each other behind his back, especially Betsy Newman. Betsy was the quintessential California girl, blond and blue-eyed, lithe and suntanned, blessed with centerfold measurements—Jessica never stood next to her if she could help it.

Raitt rattled the ice in the plastic bag. "Let's find a bench with a footrest, Jess."

"Dammit, Raitt, you aren't—"

"You're not listening again," he admonished, then appealed to the team. "Is Jess always this obstinate?"

"I can't see why, today," Betsy said, her eyes measuring every inch of Raitt's chest. "Pink is my favorite color."

"Mine, too," Raitt said, looking at Jessica. "Jess wore pink last night. Bowled me over."

Dreading that he would elaborate and tell everyone exactly how she'd sprained her ankle, she postponed her protest and hastily led him to an unoccupied picnic table.

"You're making a true pest of yourself," she grumbled, positioning her leg along the bench as he directed.

He applied the pack. "Can I buy you a cold beer?"

"Go race a turtle, instead. Play baseball or Ping-Pong. There's even a dogcart and pony ride, if you're missing old, faithful Cody."

"I'd miss arguing with you more, Jess." He sat down facing her across the table. "What don't you like about me, by the way?"

"I don't like the way we're being set up and forced together. Do you?"

"I've decided to reserve judgment until I know you better. So far, you've proven to be quite a—" he paused meaningfully "—handful."

She crossed her arms over her chest. "Let's forget this morning ever happened, all right? It was just a barnyard thing."

"It was more than animal lust, Jess. Be as honest about it as you've been about everything else."

"I'd honestly love that cold beer now, if you're still buying."

Anything to send him away so she could blush in private. The way he kept glancing at the stretchy neckline of her embroidered blouse made her feel half-undressed.

He chuckled and got to his feet. "Quite a handful," he repeated.

Watching him walk away, Jessica breathed a sigh of relief and secret longing. Betsy Newman had every reason on earth to adore pink today. Female heads were turning all over the place as Prince Raitt strode to the beer barrel. His hair glinted golden under the sun, and nothing about him was anything a woman couldn't like. Heaven forbid that he should ever divine what fantasies his hostess had been having about him ever since she'd fallen off the step.

She noticed that Betsy had apparently developed a sudden thirst and abandoned the volleyball game to join Raitt at the barrel. Women probably mobbed him even worse when he was on Cody, in his police uniform. Jessica felt like yelling to Betsy, *He's down on marriage!*

But then, Betsy wouldn't mind that the way Jessica did. Betsy had been married twice already and was now single again. At that moment, as Raitt handed the lady a beer, Jessica loathed her blond teammate. He was laughing at something she'd said. He was ogling her awesome twin peaks.

Jessica squeezed her eyes shut, imagining how Raitt would outbid everyone else for Betsy's basket. He'd Texas two-step her all over the dance pavilion tonight under the paper lanterns. Later, he'd kiss her under the stars and get two, huge handfuls of—

"Regular or light? Take your pick."

Jessica opened her eyes. Raitt was setting two, frosty brown bottles up on the table in front of her. Betsy wasn't glued to his side. She was still standing at the beer barrel, looking dumbfounded. Raitt had left her there? Alone?

Jessica curled her fingers around the light beer. "This one's fine. Unless you prefer it to the other."

"Naw. I go either way as long as it's ice-cold. What were you doing while I was gone? Having a catnap?"

"More or less." She blinked away the lingering image of his hands cradling Betsy's major assets.

He looked concerned. "Your sprain is wearing you out, I'll bet. I've been thinking you should have an X-ray. Nothing felt broken last night, but there might be a hairline fracture I couldn't detect." He glanced around. "Any doctors in the crowd here?"

"Just one. Speak of the devil." She saw old Doc Coulter coming straight toward the table; he must have spied the ice pack—and the prospect of an examination fee—through his wire-rimmed bifocals.

"Jessie, what's this I hear about you and a sprain?" Doc demanded. "Why didn't you call me to come out and look at it?"

"We had guests." She gestured across the table. "Raitt Marlow—an emergency aid expert. Doc Coulter."

"Ah. Vangie's grandson, the mounted patrolman." Doc shook Raitt's hand. "Fine woman, your grandmother. Dunc will get some stiff competition from me for her picnic basket."

Raitt said, "I was just telling Jess to get X-rayed, for safety's sake."

Doc nodded. "I agree." He pointed across the square. "My office is right over there. Let's go."

Ordinarily, Jessica would have argued against excess radiation, but now she saw a way to escape Raitt and give him an equal opportunity to escape her. She hated feeling that he'd been squiring her around out of a sense of duty to Vangie and Dunc. It couldn't have been easy for him to walk away from Betsy.

"Whatever you say, Doc." She grabbed her crutches. "See ya later, Raitt."

Raitt stood. "I'll come along."

"Not necessary," she assured him, following the doctor.

"I'm not listening, Jess." Raitt picked up both beers and brought up the rear, ignoring the glare she threw him over her shoulder.

It occurred to him that he was acting awfully solicitous—almost like a husband—for a man who had decided to reserve judgment on Jess Patton. He told himself it was one good way to stay out of Betsy Newman's clutches. She hadn't been the least bit subtle about asking him to buy her a beer.

A touch of subtlety would have been a lot more attractive. Besides, Betsy was all too aware of her charms, too eager to display them, right under a man's nose. Jess was much more of a challenge, for a multitude of complex reasons. He hadn't become a cop because he liked things simple or easy.

He waited for her in the doctor's outer office, leafed through a magazine and thought about his sex life. It had been so marginal lately that he'd gone nuclear in the stable with Jess. Her own flash fire of a response had practically melted his fly buttons.

"Just a sprain," Doc Coulter pronounced, ushering Jess into the outer office. "You'll be a lot better tomorrow if you go light on your feet today, Jessie. See that she does, Raitt. No dancing tonight."

"Yes, sir."

"Raitt has no say over what I do," Jessica impatiently advised them. "How much do I owe you for proving what I already knew, Doc?"

"I'll send you a bill. Meantime, I've got a phone call to make. Get out of here and enjoy the fun with your young man."

Raitt held the door open for her. "Thanks, Doc. Nice meeting you."

Doc waved. "No dancing," he cautioned again.

Outside, Jessica fumed, "Doc knows I never dance. No one ever—"

She caught herself, chagrined at almost revealing that no one ever asked her to dance at the town picnic. Or anywhere else, either. Budd, so long ago, didn't count.

"I'd ask you to dance, if you could," Raitt said. Had he guessed what she'd almost blurted out?

"Thank you, but I wouldn't accept."

"Why?" Raitt looked offended. "What's wrong with me?"

"You're putting me on about asking me to dance. Just like Doc was laying it on about you being my 'young man,'" she scoffed, losing her tenuous grip on her patience. Everyone seemed to be outnumbering her today, one way or another. "The whole town, including you, knows I'm an old maid who never turned a man's head in my life. 'Young man,' my eye!"

"Cut it out, Jess. Self-pity isn't your style."

She tossed her head. "What could you know about my style in the twenty-four hours you've known me, Raitt Marlow? Not much!"

Raitt watched her ponytail swing in sassy, sexy arcs as she stalked away on her crutches. He didn't follow in her wake, or call after her.

He decided to bide his time before showing Jess he knew more about her than she seemed to suspect.

6

THE AUCTION for the picnic baskets began in alphabetical order at suppertime. Both Marlow and Newman came before Patton, and long before Vangie's basket came up for bidding, Jessica was thinking that a stroll to the other side of town would be nice.

As she'd intended, Raitt had avoided her after the X-ray exam. She had covertly kept track of him, however, and knew that he'd played baseball and hit three home runs. He'd played Ping-Pong and aced the tournament. He'd lost a dollar bet with Dunc on a turtle that had never moved past the starting line. News traveled fast at a small-town picnic.

As soon as the auction began, he stopped avoiding her. "Having fun?" he asked, walking up when the auctioneer announced the first basket.

She stifled a mock yawn. "Oh, yes. Such great fun to sit in one place all day with one foot higher than the other. And you?"

"I'm hungry."

Jessica didn't find that surprising, since Raitt had just come off a short stint on the volleyball court. His eyes looked strained from watching Betsy serve the ball.

"Betsy's basket never comes cheap," she murmured.

"Yeah? Big bucks?"

She nodded. "Three figures."

Raitt took out his wallet and checked the cash compartment. "Do they take checks and credit cards?"

"They'll take any form of money, bar none," Dunc said, joining them. He and Vangie were hand in hand, smiling, blindingly happy.

Jessica saw every hope of a crosstown stroll evaporate, then saw that the women's rest room wasn't far away. Even though the line of people waiting looked long. If she got into it right now, she might luck out and be incognito by the time her basket entered the bidding. She could just stay in there until Dunc bought it. That ploy had worked two years out of the last three.

She laid a hand on her crutches and got a hard look from Dunc. He leaned over and muttered, "No duckin' out on me this year, gal. Mind yer manners."

"What a perfect day," Vangie was saying to Raitt. "I remember days—and auctions—like this in Texas."

Vangie kept up a steady stream of chat, punctuating it with enthusiastic applause each time a basket sold, and Jessica steeled herself for the inevitable.

Soon Vangie's basket was on the block. Bidding was brisk among the three town widowers—Dunc, Doc Coulter and the mayor. Dunc outbid them all, of course, to Vangie's obvious delight.

When he went forward to claim his win, Raitt ambled away to the beer barrel. Watching him, Jessica heard the auctioneer say, "Betsy Newman's basket."

Bids rang out from everywhere at once. The bachelors around town clearly craved a picnic with a spectacular view. Jessica closed her eyes and listened for Raitt's bid.

"Fifty," she heard his deep voice call out.

"Fifty-five," someone else countered.

A third eager swain offered, "Sixty."

Jess knew it would go for over a hundred dollars. It always did. Three times as much as the other baskets. She listened again for Raitt. How high would he go?

"Regular or light?"

She opened her eyes and saw him standing in front of her with two more beers, while bidders right and left drove up the price of the basket of choice.

"Going once...going twice..." the auctioneer warned.

"Regular or light, Jess?"

Was Raitt deaf? Didn't he hear the last call?

"Sold!" the auctioneer declared.

"Jess, I can't drink them both. Take your pick. Where does the bid stand right now? Seventy-five and rising?"

"One hundred fifty dollars." Jessica picked the regular this time. "You just lost."

"I did?" Raitt snapped his fingers. "Damn."

"Jessie's basket's next," Dunc advised.

"Great," Raitt responded, folding his arms over his chest.

Great, she thought, wishing there were some way she could levitate out of town. Up, up and away she'd rise. Back to the ranch, the horses, the cattle, the chickens, the only comfort zone she'd ever known.

"Jessica Patton's basket," the auctioneer announced.

Dunc immediately offered his standard bid. "Fifty dollars."

The auctioneer tipped his cowboy hat in acknowledgment. "I'vegotfiftygimmefifty-five."

All for a good cause, Jessica reminded herself. *Guzzle beer and pretend you couldn't care less who bids how much for what.*

"Two hundred dollars," Raitt called.

Everyone gasped and the crowd froze, mouths open, eyes wide, disbelief on every face. Jessica froze, too, staring at Raitt.

"Sold!"

Raitt turned a dazzling, triumphant smile to her. "All mine, Jess."

"That's what I call a Texas bid!" whooped Dunc, slapping Raitt on the back.

Still stunned, Jessica watched Raitt stride forward to claim his supper. *Two hundred dollars!* She had an instant recall of Rhett Butler rendering a crowd speechless with a similar bid for one dance with Scarlett O'Hara.

A hubbub erupted, everyone talking at once and glancing from Raitt to Jessica. She realized he'd returned with the basket and was taking her beer out of her frozen hand, saying, "Let's eat over there under that tree."

Too dazed to argue or object, she took up her crutches and followed his lead. Behind her, she heard the auctioneer directing everyone's attention to the next basket on the block. He had to repeat the donor's name three times before there was a bid.

She sat on the park bench Raitt had chosen. He sat right next to her with the basket and watched her face slowly become suffused with color. It wasn't a blush. She was thawing out. He braced himself.

She began to sputter. "Two *hundred* dollars—"

"It's a good cause, Jess."

"If Granddad bribed you—"

"*I* paid for it. My idea." It didn't explain why he'd done it. He couldn't make it clear to her—or himself—why he'd taken rash, romantic action in such a flamboyant, public way.

"You pity me," she accused, her voice shaking with anger and humiliation. "Granddad told you no one ever buys my basket but him, so you—"

"I wanted it," Raitt cut in. "I got it. If you don't want to share it with me, you can buy it back at full price —plus a fifty-percent disappointment fee."

"Disappointed?" she scoffed. "You?"

"Jess, why do I always get an argument from you, no matter what I say or do? Why can't we just eat ribs and chili in peace here? Huh?"

"Disappointed," she scoffed again, but not half as vehemently as before.

"I like you, Jess." *Nothing more, nothing less,* It was just an auction, and he was just another hungry man. He opened the basket and took out a container of strawberries. "Relax."

Jess couldn't quite obey. "I didn't prepare anything in this basket. You only bought it because I—"

Raitt poked a huge, scarlet strawberry into her open mouth. "Shut up and give me my money's worth." He poised another berry, clearly ready to keep her quiet.

Jessica subsided and chewed her sweet mouthful in silence. She'd never forget the awed gasp from the crowd. Surely Raitt had heard it and realized what it meant? No one would have blinked twice if he had bid the same amount for Betsy's basket. They might have elbowed each other in the ribs, but nothing more than that.

She looked at Raitt and saw him looking at Betsy. Betsy's basket beau, a truck mechanic, was also focusing on her.

"She must spend a lot on hair bleach," Raitt observed, returning his gaze to Jessica. "I like your hair better." *Better and better,* he realized, wishing he could honestly think otherwise.

Jessica handled his compliment like a hot potato. "Well, mine's natural, if nothing else."

"My girlfriend in high school had dark hair like yours," Raitt recalled. "She dumped me in favor of the student body president."

"Hard to believe," Jessica muttered. She couldn't imagine any normal female would dump Raitt Marlow.

He started bringing food out of the basket. The menu was barbecued ribs, chili in a thermos jug, corn bread and jalapeño jelly, jumbo strawberries.

The sun set as they ate. Paper lanterns strung in the trees came on and cast a soft glow. A country and western band assembled in the dance pavilion and struck up a Roy Orbison classic, "Pretty Woman." Naturally, Betsy led that dance with the brawny mechanic. Then Dunc requested "Yellow Rose of Texas," and whirled Vangie onto the dance floor.

Jessica saw them smooching as they waltzed. She popped the last strawberry into her mouth and tried to enjoy it. Dunc had never smooched with Lizbeth on the dance floor like that. He'd never paid as much for Lizbeth's basket as he'd paid today for Vangie's, either. Lizbeth must be turning over under her tombstone.

"Would you waltz with me if you could?" Raitt inquired, sliding his arm along the back of the park bench.

She almost choked on the strawberry. "I never dance, as you already know."

"I paid a lot to be the first to ask, Jess."

She leaned forward, away from his arm and the way it was warming her shoulders and melting her spine. "Granddad and Vangie are making a spectacle of themselves. Look."

"I've noticed." He was noticing other things, as well. How Jess's dark hair and lightly tanned skin reflected the soft lantern glow. How her slender fingers toyed nervously with the elastic neckline of her blouse. How her perfume was very faint now, tantalizing him very subtly. He touched her shoulder.

"They're leaving the dance floor, Raitt. The waltz isn't even over. They're—look at them, slipping away to the parking lot. What are they up to now?"

Any other time, Vangie's welfare would have been uppermost in his mind. Now it seemed much less important than being with Jess. He could only think he'd done well to choose the park bench in the shadows, where he and Jess were a bit removed from the evening activities.

He loved the country scents in the evening air, liked having Jess to himself. Baiting her. Teasing her. He was curious to see if she'd soften and respond to the romantic music, the starry summer night—to him.

A strolling concessioner came by with a rustic barrow full of flowers. "A posy for the lady, sir?"

"Every gardenia you've got," Raitt replied, pulling out his wallet.

"Three in all."

"Sold." Raitt paid and took the three exotic blossoms. He presented them to Jess, who hadn't uttered a word of protest. "Don't tell me you never accept flowers from your admirers."

She wasn't about to tell him she'd never received flowers, aside from the embroidered poppies on her blouse. His spontaneous gift was making her forget whatever it was Dunc and Vangie were doing among the parked cars.

The flowers were a first for her. Even though Raitt had to be doing it under grand-parental duress, she couldn't make herself resist her first gift of flowers from a man. Especially from Raitt.

"They're beautiful. Thank you."

He tucked all three into her ponytail, then framed her face in her hands. "You're more than welcome, Miss Jess."

She felt faint at the idea that he might kiss her. His face was so close that she could hear and feel each breath he took. Hot, moist, husky. Now his finger-tips were tracing the shape of her ears, the line of her jaw, and he was whispering her name.

"Jess . . . you smell so good. Look at me. . . ."

Look? How, without going cross-eyed? His lips were coming nearer, nearer. Oh, bliss, his fingers were stroking her throat, outlining her collarbones. She flattened her palms against his chest to dissuade him, but found no strength to push. Instead she found the smooth texture of his knit shirt and the solid plane of muscle it covered.

"Miss Jess . . ." he whispered once more. Then he kissed her as a woman should be kissed on a balmy summer evening. Gently, seductively at first, until she wanted his tongue sliding between her lips, until she surrendered her tongue in return.

Powerful urges swept through him, earthy and erotic, as he enclosed Jess in his arms and feasted on her delicious mouth. She was just what he wanted to hold and kiss and taste. He'd had many women, but never one like Jess, so starved for attention that her response was an instant turn-on.

He drew back a little when he realized how profoundly Jess was affecting him. His muscles were tense, taut, almost quivering with desire, and there was no question of how far he was ready to go with her. Too far to go on a park bench in public.

Shocked, thrilled and dismayed, Jessica emerged from Raitt's lengthy kiss and wriggled out of his loosening embrace. As she lurched to her feet, several things occurred to her all at once. Raitt had kissed her out of sheer boredom. Or maybe because he'd paid big and gotten stuck with her and the basket. She had kissed Raitt because she couldn't help herself around a man like him.

Now she couldn't run away fast enough. "Time to pack it in and drive home," she advised him breathlessly, snatching up her crutches. "Go find Granddad and Vangie. Heaven only knows what they're doing that no one at their age should do."

"Jess, calm down. And give me a moment to, er, adjust my own attitude."

Dizzy, she leaned hard on her crutches to steady herself. Twice in one day she had somehow ended up French-kissing Raitt with foolish eagerness and adolescent abandon. She couldn't blame him for being bored, but blaming herself was easy. She had been a fool for Budd, hadn't she? Had any man ever been a fool for Jessica Patton? Never.

The sensuous perfume of fresh gardenias surrounded her, and she felt herself tremble. It was past time to go home.

"Hurry up, Raitt."

"Down is the direction I'm aiming for," he retorted. "What's your hurry?"

"Our grandparents are out in the parking lot— parking. They hardly know each other, much less anything about safe sex."

Raitt found the idea of Vangie having unsafe sex deflating enough to enable him to stand up straight without great cause for embarrassment. Nonetheless, he risked reinflation by taking Jess into his arms again and kissing her long and hard to teach her a lesson.

"Don't ever think you can order me around, Jess," he warned, then stalked off to seek out Dunc and Vangie.

What was so damned attractive and arousing about sharp-tongued Jessica Patton? Raitt angrily asked himself on the way to the parking lot. Two kisses. Why had he sought them? Past a certain point, his kisses had apparently not been what Jess wanted.

Worse, they hadn't been in his own best interest. What a mess!

He checked his car and found it empty. If the grandparents weren't parked like a couple of teenagers, where were they? A thick clump of bushes bordered one side of the parking area. Raitt wandered over and detected heavy breathing behind one bush.

"Dunc? Vangie? What are you doing in the bushes?"

"Nothin'," an out-of-breath teenage voice replied. "We're not doin' nothin', man."

Raitt could imagine how much "nothin'" the boy was engaged in with his girlfriend. He imagined himself hidden in the same bushes, enjoying similar guilty pleasures with Jess.

Shaking his head to clear it of unwanted thoughts, Raitt returned to the park bench and found Jessica and the basket, packed and ready to leave.

"No sign of them in lovers' lane," he told her.

"I'll flush them out," she said. Sticking two fingers into her mouth, she blew a piercing, three-note whistle. "An emergency call Granddad taught me when I was little. A lot like dialing 911."

Sure enough, Dunc and Vangie appeared less than a minute later, flushed and breathless.

"What's the problem, gal?"

"Time to go home. My ankle has had it." In truth, it was feeling a lot better, but they didn't have to know.

On the way to the car, Dunc handed the keys to Raitt and said, "Fair's fair. Vangie and I'll take to the backseat for the return trip."

Raitt didn't like that idea at all, for two reasons. One, his grandmother would be all over Dunc back there, or vice versa. Two, Jess would have her own, separate seat up front.

But then, wouldn't that be best? he asked himself, knowing he should feel relief rather than regret at Dunc's suggestion. Yes. Relief was the right response for a man who had no intention of getting any more than sexually involved in his relationships.

Unlike him, Jess was the marrying type. He suspected she'd give her whole heart if she fell in love, just as she gave wholehearted love and loyalty to her grandfather. Instinct warned that she'd expect marriage once she opened her heart, whereas he was never, ever going to get married.

"The back's a tight squeeze for two people," he said in token discouragement.

Dunc grinned at Vangie, who said, "That's the big idea."

Despite his deepest instincts, despite every wise self-warning, Raitt drove away, envying the grandparents their tight squeeze.

7

JESSICA WOKE AT DAWN the next day to the sound of two people sneaking stealthily out the back door. She showered quickly and reached the kitchen just in time to see Dunc and Vangie riding toward the sunrise together on Marcus and Aunt Lucille, followed by Murph and Muttley. Dunc had scrawled a note, saying the morning chores were done.

Raitt came in as she was witnessing their escape. He watched, too, frowning and recalling the comment Vangie had made on the way home last night. "Now I know," she had rhapsodized, "what love at first sight is." Dunc had seconded that notion.

"I don't believe in love at first sight," Jessica grumbled grimly.

"I don't, either," Raitt muttered. "They're acting positively juvenile."

"Someone should ride out after them and baby-sit."

"Your ankle is in no shape to ride."

"It's one crutch better than yesterday." She limped on her single support to the coffee maker, began measuring out enough for a full pot, and suggested, "You could ride out on Teardrop and catch up with them. She's not too pregnant yet for a ride."

Raitt sighed. "Unfortunately, our grandparents aren't children."

"They're not acting like adults, Raitt. Playing with fire, as we both know."

"Not like us," he said wryly, "unless you count two kisses as childish."

"Childish and best forgotten," she added. "You didn't mean anything by either one, and neither did I."

Raitt disliked feeling as unrested and grumpy as he felt this morning. He'd woken up fully aroused the minute Jess turned on the shower. Something about the image of her stepping under the spray was enough to torture him with every sexual fantasy imaginable. Now, Jess's words only made his black mood blacker.

"*I* meant something by it," he growled, "whether you did or not. I don't kiss just anyone I come across."

Jess plugged in the coffee maker. "A lot of men lose their bearings when they're hard up for the pleasures of the big city. San Francisco, for instance."

"You know what's wrong with you, Jess?" He clamped a hand on her shoulder and turned her to face him. "You don't give yourself any credit at all."

She gave him a withering glare, pulled out of his hold, and blurted, "Neither did Budd Cochran."

"Well, I'm not Butt Cockroach, in case you haven't noticed." He gripped her hand and pumped it up and down in an exaggerated handshake. "Raitt Marlow, ma'am. Mighty pleased to meet you. What's for breakfast?"

"Nothing, if you don't stop this silliness!" Although Raitt had provoked her beyond patience, she had to surrender the shadow of a smile to him for his apt reference to Budd. Budd had been a heavy cigarette smoker, puffing carton after carton down to the butts.

"I didn't start this argument, Jess. You did." Raitt's tone softened. "Hey, is that a smile I see on the same lips I kissed last night?"

"A small one," she allowed more calmly. "He *was* the lowest form of insect."

"Want to tell me about it?"

"Not really."

She pushed it all back to a distant corner of her heart. It was far more comforting to focus on Raitt's softer tone and expression. He looked and sounded genuinely concerned and willing to listen, traits that she could see were probably very beneficial to the street kids he encountered on his San Francisco beat. They must love him.

"Okay, don't," he agreed. "But note one thing—a kiss from me indicates a certain amount of honest interest. I'm not the same species of insect Butt was."

"Budd," Jessica corrected, unable to ignore the fact that Raitt still had hold of her hand; she wanted to know what that and his words really meant. Curiosity won out. "Interest in what, Raitt?"

"You know what, Jess. Nothing serious. Just natural, mutual attraction with no strings or expectations attached. We're both old enough to—"

She clenched the hand he was holding. "I'm not here for any man's personal relief."

Raitt let her hand go. "I'm not assuming that you are. If you're interested, we can enjoy each other. If not . . ."

Jessica hadn't expected Raitt to equal her own candor. She couldn't say with total honesty, "I'm not interested," since it wasn't true and her response to his kisses couldn't have escaped his notice. At the moment, oblique dishonesty seemed to be the best policy.

"What if I'm not interested?"

"You're welcome to convince me, Jess. I can take a big enough hint."

Raitt knew he should be taking the biggest hint from his own intuition. It was telling him to back off, that staying emotionally uninvolved with Jessica Patton wouldn't be easy. But as he looked at her fresh, clean-scrubbed face, a different inner voice insisted it could be done.

All it would require was finesse as well as frankness, up front. Since he couldn't be any more forthright with her than he'd just been, that left finesse. A man with his years of experience was long on know-how.

Jessica turned away and opened the refrigerator. "Are scrambled eggs all right with you?"

"Not if you don't sit down and let me scramble them. Rest your sprain, or I'll call Doc Coulter to come out and examine you again."

"Honestly, Raitt, you're the bossiest, most infuriat—"

"I'll call, Jess," he cut in, glancing at the kitchen phone. "I'm not bluffing."

For the first time in her life, she flounced across a room. It wasn't easy on one crutch. And for the first time she understood why females flounced—nonviolent protest against male brutes.

She grabbed the newspaper and read it closely until Raitt put a plate of eggs and toast in front of her. "Thank you." Keeping the paper propped up against her juice glass, she avoided his eyes as he poured coffee for her.

He ate his own breakfast standing up, looking through the window above the sink. It was another sunny day, warm with a slight breeze from the west. Jessica peeked at him over the paper, noticing how his jeans molded the shape of his tight rear. Long before that, she had noticed that they also molded everything in front to perfection.

"So what do you think?" he inquired after he'd finished eating and rinsed off his plate.

Her thoughts were riveted on his five-button fly. She gulped. "About what?"

"Natural, mutual attraction. Enjoying ourselves."

Jessica got up on her crutch immediately. "I have a stack of bills to pay, guest towels to wash, bread to bake and lunch for four to prepare. Entertain yourself."

Peeved by her brusque dismissal, Raitt went out to visit the horses. Then the chickens. Then the garden toolshed.

Indoors, Jessica wrote several checks and balanced the ranch ledger to the last penny. She washed, dried and folded bath towels, showing no partiality to the towel that had absorbed every shower drop on Raitt's eye-catching body two mornings in a row.

She was in the kitchen, kneading bread dough, when she heard the lawn mower start up. Raitt came into view through the kitchen window, guiding the mower across the back lawn to the side. He moved out of sight and she punched the dough with frustrated oomph.

At least he's making himself useful. It made her think of how useful he had offered to be to her earlier. *Natural, mutual attraction.* Sex, plain and simple, was what he'd meant, precisely what Budd had shared with her years ago. Just that. Nothing more.

If Raitt brought it up again, she'd inform him that she could manage her own needs herself. Millions of women did, in case he hadn't read the sex statistics today's newspapers reported. "Truly safe sex." An enlightened Peoria minister had even been quoted as preaching on that touchy subject.

She heard the mower stop. Raitt came in and poured himself a glass of ice water from a pitcher in the fridge.

"Hot out there," he said, stripping off his shirt and going out again.

Jessica pinned her eyes on the bread dough and felt a jolt of solar-hot desire sizzle down her spine. This was how a mare in season must feel. Restless. Aching. Melting in every secret, female nook and cranny.

She looked up and saw Raitt steer the mower onto the back lawn. His shoulders and biceps gleamed with sweat. As she had imagined, the hair on his chest was thick, as golden as a wheat field in August, as tempting to touch as the hair on his head.

Feverish with unstoppable erotic fantasies, she kneaded dough and watched Raitt mow. She didn't glance away or realize that she'd overworked the bread until Dunc and Vangie came trotting back from their ride and led their horses into the stable.

Jessica was setting the table for lunch when they came in. Raitt came in, too, and disappeared to wash up. She put out assorted cold cuts, two salads and a medley of melon balls. Raitt reappeared and took his seat at the table.

"Worked up an appetite, I see," Dunc said after thanking him for his hard work.

Raitt nodded and filled his plate. "I needed some exercise. Jess got some, too, kneading bread."

"It didn't proof," she mumbled, rubbing her aching arms. "Bad yeast." She'd make sure Raitt was nowhere in sight the next time she baked.

"Things were proofin' real nice out on the sunrise trail," said Dunc roguishly, making eyes at Vangie.

Vangie's eyes twinkled. "I'll hate to leave here when my visit is over."

"Don't have to leave permanently if you don't want to," Dunc huskily assured her.

Jessica stared at the pimento center of a green olive, embedded in a slice of lunch meat on her own plate. Granddad sounded too certain of what he was saying. He was practically proposing marriage, for heaven's sake, after only two days of knowing this woman.

"Grandma Lizbeth always said 'Time will tell,' Granddad."

Dunc fixed a bristle-browed gaze upon her. "I've been tellin' Vangie all about Lizbeth and the special wisdom she had. Likewise, Vangie's filled me in on her Leland's special ways. Nobody's forgettin' anybody in the past, the way you might think, gal."

"Jess has a valid point, though," Raitt put in. "Both sides of the Marlow family have learned the lesson in the old adage about marrying in haste and repenting in sorrow."

Surprised that he had come to her defense, Jessica thanked him with her eyes. He acknowledged her thanks the same way and she felt a sudden, close kinship with him.

"You two haven't lived long enough to tell two old folks a hell of a lot about time," Dunc retorted mildly.

"Amen," Vangie agreed.

The phone rang and Dunc reached for it. "Howdy." He listened for a few moments. "Yes. Right here." Covering the receiver, he said to Raitt, "Your mounted patrol boss. Take it in the front room if you want your privacy."

"Thanks. I will."

Dunc hung up the phone after Raitt picked up at the other end. "His boss didn't sound real happy to me."

"Oh, dear." Vangie sighed. "I hope it's not about more budget cuts. The patrol can't survive on a shoe-string. Raitt is already on forced leave because of prior cuts. He wouldn't be here with me otherwise."

Dunc gave her a teasing grin. "Still think you need a chaperon, Mrs. Marlow?"

"Only my big, strong grandson thought I needed one. I knew you were an honorable man, Duncan, from the moment I heard your voice on the tele-phone."

Duncan? Jessica refrained from rolling her eyes. If his cronies could hear this, they'd crow like roosters.

Raitt returned to the table and grimly delivered some bad news. "Another budget cut. The patrol won't ride again for six months. I have two options: transfer to a desk job or remain on leave without pay."

Vangie looked stricken. "You'll hate a desk job."

"Tell me about it. I'd almost rather stay on leave until the city decides in six months whether this cut is going to be temporary or permanent."

"Can you afford to stay on leave?"

He shrugged. "Not beyond a six-month comfort zone. By then my savings will be shot." He shook his head. "The chief says our horses will be farmed out to a few stables generous enough to donate stalls and horse feed."

"Oh, Raitt." Vangie's dark eyes were sympathetic. "Cody farmed out to strangers?"

Dunc slapped the table. "Horsefeathers, boy. Bring Cody up here, if they'll let you. My stable's half-empty from what it used to be. Move yourself up here and be my temporary ranch hand while you're laid off," he added expansively. "That'll solve your immediate problems till the city budget works itself out."

Jessica blinked, unable to believe that Dunc was making such an offer without consulting her first. In matters to do with work she was an equal partner with him. He'd always consulted her on important matters. Always, until now. Now he was way out of line.

"Granddad, Raitt is a policeman, not a ranch hand. He knows nothing about cattle."

"He knows the basics," Vangie interjected. "How many summers did you spend on the Texas ranch where I grew up, Raitt? Ten, at least."

"Raitt can learn whatever he missed along the way," Dunc said.

"What about looking for horse patrol work in a different city?" Jessica persisted.

"There aren't that many patrols across the nation. Wherever they exist, there are mile-long waiting lists for those jobs."

"No use lookin' elsewhere till the city decides for good in six months," said Dunc.

"Granddad, we don't need a—"

"Jessie, we've been needin' a strong hand for a good long time here. How do you vote, Raitt? Desk jockey or cowboy?"

Raitt aimed a sidelong look at Jess and she shook her head in candid discouragement. Then he looked at Vangie, who nodded vigorously.

"Sorry, Jess," he said, then clasped Dunc's outstretched hand in a firm handshake. "Cowboy."

Jessica sat back in her chair, outnumbered, outvoted, facing a future that had changed in a heartbeat. Six months loomed ahead, with Raitt Marlow underfoot every minute of every month!

8

RAITT DROVE DUNC'S PICKUP and horse trailer to San Francisco the next day. It was a long drive, giving him hours to think. Jess occupied the center of his thoughts. That disturbed him.

He'd gotten a little too caught up with her, too interested in everything that made her tick. Getting back to San Francisco would defuse the unexpected interest and widen his focus again.

He planned the week ahead as he drove. He'd prepare his apartment for his six-month absence, tie up the odds and ends of his city life, load Cody into the trailer, then head back to the ranch to begin his life as a cowboy.

He decided to call a flight attendant he sometimes dated. She enjoyed being taken out to dinner in Chinatown. What was more, she'd invite him to spend every night of the week in her bed, with no strings attached.

That way, he'd get a few things out of his system and restore his neutral outlook on women and relationships. When he returned to the ranch, he'd give Betsy Newman a call and play the casual dating game with her, too. No misunderstandings, no broken hearts, no regrets.

JESSICA HADN'T KNOWN a week could be so long. It took ages for the day of Raitt's return to arrive. She woke every morning, expecting to hear Raitt in the next room, then realized again that he was gone. Her bathroom and her time were all hers, but nothing seemed the same.

She would have liked to take Dunc to task for overriding her about Raitt, but she could never get a moment alone with Granddad. He and Vangie were carrying on like lovebirds. After a few days Jessica had to admit that Vangie was probably everything Dunc needed in a woman and a wife. Day by day it grew a little less difficult for her to accept Vangie's cheerful presence and positive influence on her grandfather.

They were madly, crazily, merrily in love. Dunc announced the fact one night at the dinner table—as if anyone needed to be told.

The only really good thing about the week was that her ankle recovered. On the day Raitt was scheduled to return, she came in for lunch and found Dunc and Vangie packing their suitcases.

"Where are you going?"

"Frisco," Dunc replied. "Vangie wants me to meet her friends and more of her family besides Raitt. From there, we'll head down to L.A., so she can get acquainted with your folks and sister."

"When did all this get planned?"

"Between the sheets last night, if you get my drift."

"Granddad!"

He eyed her over the lid of his suitcase. "Stop starin' bug-eyed, like you never heard of sex after sixty. A natural fact of life, sex is." His eyes twinkled. "And fun, too—specially at our age."

Jessica closed her mouth, but not for long. "If Raitt finds out, he'll—"

"He's why we're leavin' as soon as he gets back here. I don't want to go twelve rounds with him about who sleeps in what bed from now on. His face is too handsome to mash up over the facts of life. Don't you go tattlin' to him, either, gal."

"Granddad, you can't leave me here all alone with a strange man."

"You *need* to be alone with a man, for a change, Jessie. Raitt's a decent, law-abiding fella who's got his head screwed on straight. Maybe he'll put a twinkle back in your eye like Vangie has for me."

Jessica didn't waste any more breath. She stomped out of his bedroom, knowing he'd drive off with his new bedmate, no one could stop him. But she was damned if she was going to stand on the porch and wave goodbye to such deserters.

She was in the stable, saddling Aunt Lucille for a long ride, when the dogs started barking. She heard Dunc's pickup truck drive into the yard. Raitt. Then came the sound of him backing up the trailer to the stable entrance.

"Suck it in, Lucille," she ordered as she tightened the saddle cinch around the mare.

Outside, in the mares' section of the horse pasture, Teardrop started nickering one tone lower than usual. Jessica identified it as the mare's Raitt Marlow nicker, a throaty love call. Alamo, in his own paddock, neighed loudly. It was stud against stud, a challenge for supremacy.

Jessica didn't turn when Raitt entered the stable with the dogs joyfully leading the way. She heard the sound of his boots approaching on the creaky wooden floor, then stop. Murph yipped to catch her attention.

"I'm back," Raitt said. "Do I still have a job here?"

"Not if you've been intelligent enough to change your mind." She continued to adjust the cinch. "Suck in another inch, Luce."

"Miss me at all?" he murmured gruffly.

"No more than you missed me." Heart galloping, fingers fumbling with the cinch buckle, she braced herself to turn and face him.

"You're making me feel real welcome with your back to me like that, Jess."

She turned and met his gaze. It was narrow, blue and wry under the low brim of his cowboy hat.

"I've never been the welcoming committee around here," she said, lowering the brim of her own hat to shut him out again.

"Where's the committee?"

"Inside, packing their suitcases for a meet-the-in-laws trip to San Francisco and L.A. They'll be leaving any minute now." *Leaving me here alone, with you.*

"Trip? Since when?"

"Ask them, not me. They've got minds of their own and seem to have lost both of them." She paused, hearing a car door slam. "That's them, making their getaway."

Raitt spun on one boot heel and strode out of the stable toward Dunc's sedan. Murph and Muttley scrambled to keep up with him. Watching from the stable door, Jessica saw Dunc close the trunk as Raitt approached. Both men began to gesture. Their voices rose. The dogs came slinking back to the stable, tails between their legs, as if the argument were about them.

Then Vangie came out of the house, dressed to travel and clearly ready to go. She and Dunc got into the car and drove off, leaving Raitt choking on driveway dust.

Jessica heaved a weary sigh, knowing just how frustrated and helpless he was feeling. She had felt the same way all week; Dunc and Vangie's constant billing and cooing had left her feeling like a third wheel every blessed day and night.

He came back to the stable cursing under his breath. Jessica nodded, in perfect agreement with the stream of rancorous words.

"You can say that again."

"They act like they've been sleeping together. Have they?" He was really seething.

She didn't give their secret away. "There's no one to stop them now." Returning to Lucille, she double-checked the cinch.

Raitt followed. "Where are you and Lucille going?"

"To the end of the valley. She needs exercise, and part of the fence out there needs mending."

"Right this minute? Hell, this is some damned welcome I get after a whole week out of everyone's sight. Including yours, Jess."

He hadn't thought he'd miss her much. But he had, although it wasn't comfortable for him to admit it. He hadn't socialized, either, as he had planned. There had been a your-place-or-mine message on his phone recorder from the flight attendant, but the time had somehow never seemed right to dial her number and follow through.

Time had run out, and he'd spent most of it thinking about Dunc's granddaughter. But she looked and sounded unhappy to see him. Or not happy enough to show it.

"There's cold chicken in the refrigerator if you're hungry," she said. "Potato salad, too. Did you bring Cody?"

"Yeah." Too glad to see Jess again, he'd forgotten that his horse needed to be let out of the trailer. "Is any empty stall okay for him?"

"Take your pick." Anxious to leave before her feelings showed she led Aunt Lucille out of the stable and swung into the saddle.

"Stick around a minute and meet Cody," Raitt invited in an attempt to detain her. *Maybe even give me a hello hug. Or a kiss.*

"I'll meet him later when I get back."

"Fine. Don't do the hired hand and his horse any little favors, Jess," he commented curtly. Tight-lipped, he turned his back on her and headed toward the horse trailer.

JESSICA WAS REPLACING rotten fence posts with new ones when Lucille began to whinny. A whinny of welcome. Raitt rode into view on Marcus.

Startled, Jessica drew in a sharp breath. This was the first time she'd seen Raitt astride a horse. Cantering toward her he was a compelling male figure, a vivid reminder of the day he had emerged from his car in a luminous cloud of dust. Today he looked and rode like a high-plains drifter, a man in his natural element.

Lord, if there had ever been any such thing as a cowboy prince of the Western range, here he was. He rode as well as she did, confident and entirely at ease in the saddle. His thighs bulged with muscle.

Jessica almost dropped the fresh post she was positioning. She could hardly speak as he reined in Marcus and approached her.

"R-Raitt! What are you doing here?"

"Looking for work. I thought Marcus might find you. We trusted our instincts—and the main trail." He stroked the gelding's mane sensuously, letting the chestnut strands drift between his fingers. "It looks lonely out here, despite the fabulous view."

His gaze was on her, not on the long view of the valley. Under a sheen of perspiration she felt her skin prickle in response. How did he know she'd been feeling lonely?

"A fabulous view is always good company," she said. "Lucille is, too." She whistled to the dogs to return from wherever their noses had led them. "So are Murph and Muttley."

"Better than me?"

Unable to hold the post any longer, she let it slide awkwardly into the hole. "I'm used to working alone out here."

"You didn't answer the question, Jess." He secured his reins and dismounted, letting Marcus sidestep to where Aunt Lucille was grazing. "Better company than me?"

"Raitt, you know I don't agree with Granddad about you working here."

He scowled. "Let's get a few things straight. If you're really not interested in me, I'm not interested in you. If you are, maybe I am, too. Either way, I'll live."

"You'd live a lot better in the city at the desk job your boss offered you. If you had taken it, Granddad and Vangie would never have skipped out and left me alone. Knowing you'd be here, they skipped."

"Dammit, Jess, I'm not at fault for needing a job or accepting a job offer. Aren't you even slightly happy to see the only other human being in a twenty-mile radius?"

Too happy, she thought. *Budd broke my heart and robbed my pride. You'll do the same in your own way if I let down my guard. You sound and act interested, but for you to have any genuine interest in me defies all logic.*

"Granddad hired you to work here. If you rode out this way to find work, get busy, pulling out old fence posts."

He pulled a pair of Dunc's leather work gloves out of his back pocket. "I can see what needs to be done without you telling me."

"Do it, then."

"How much overtime do you expect?"

"None."

"Fine. Then again . . ." He paused, putting on the gloves. "What if I put in my own overtime to earn some respect and admiration?"

"Granddad always says a well-done job earns its own respect."

"Then maybe I'll work overtime wearing down your resistance to natural, mutual attraction," he mused. "It's a terrible thing to waste, you know."

"Speak for yourself. I learned ten years ago not to trust ranch hand sweet talk. My brain has matured since Budd."

"Ten years. A long time for your mature body to live without what a man could do for it," he retorted, picking up the shovel she'd been using. "Hold that post straight in the hole and I'll fill in the dirt."

His words reminded him how long his own mature body had been living solo. But not so long that sleeping with Jess would change his aversion to commitment, he assured himself.

"I'm none the worse for sleeping alone," she said, holding the post steady while he shoveled soil around it. "Still as plain and rawboned as I've always been. Not the stuff of any man's dreams. Nightmares, maybe."

He vigorously tamped down the dirt with the shovel handle and his boot heels. "Not beautiful inside, where it counts, Jess? Not filled with female passion and desire?"

Inflamed by Raitt's seductive inquisition, Jessica let go of the post and suppressed a momentary yearning to believe every word and welcome his gruff, insistent overture. He was the man of her secret dreams, but acknowledging her romantic longings would give Raitt all the power over her that Budd had once taken advantage of.

Raitt caught her gloved hand in his. "Answer me, Jess."

"Let go, Raitt."

Tightening his grip, he pulled her close so that she had to flatten one gloved hand against his chest, had to look up and meet his eyes. Hers had darkened to a deep, brilliant green, communicating an emotion he'd learned to identify as either anger or desire—often a mixture of both.

God help him, he wanted it to be pure desire. He wanted her to lift her lips to his and make him feel that she had missed him all week, that she welcomed his return.

"We could get along with each other if you'd let us," he murmured.

"I—" She broke off unexpectedly; the steep angle of her head had made her hat fall off. Unconfined, wisps of her dark hair blew free in the soft breeze and feathered into his chest hair where his collar lay open.

"Give peace a chance, Jess."

Even through her leather work glove she could feel how hard his chest was. His grip on her other hand remained strong, inescapable. She couldn't say he was hurting her, for she was feeling no pain. Her body was flush against his, and she felt him curl one of his legs behind one of hers at the knee.

She told herself that the interest he was displaying was purely circumstantial; after all, he was stuck on a ranch where the nearest town was an hour away by car. Such isolation would make any man rationalize that her warm body was better than nothing. One woman wasn't much different from another if a man closed his eyes.

His were closing now. He was brushing a string of kisses along her cheekbone. She heard a tiny, breathless moan and realized it was her own. Her bones seemed to be disintegrating, melting into his strength.

He rotated his hips against hers, and she moved with him.

"Damn you, Raitt," she whimpered, surrendering to the sexual motion.

"That's it, Miss Jess," he said approvingly, letting go of the shovel and pushing back his hat brim. "Cuss me and kiss me."

He tilted her chin and kissed her trembling lips until they parted and allowed his tongue to slide in and unite with hers. Swallowing her passionate sighs, he worked his hand out of the glove and touched her breast. Firm and warm, it nestled in his hand. He slipped open two of her shirt buttons, slid his fingers inside and circled them over her nipple.

"Raitt!" she gasped. "Please...you're making me..."

Drawing back slightly, he released another button and bared her breast. "I'm only making you want what you need." He strummed her swelling nipple, cherishing her response.

Breathless with pleasure, she glanced at the moving hand, saw his fingers stroking her, making her need visible. Making her feel lovely and desirable, more feminine than she'd ever felt before. Glancing up, she saw that his eyes were shut.

Shut tight! Not wide open and feasting on her face, not even focusing on her bare flesh. She tensed and grew still, felt his hand stop cruising, watched his eyes open to the realization that something had changed.

"Jess?"

She yanked her wrist out of his clasp and backed away, clutching her shirtfront. "You leave me alone, cowboy."

"What the—what did I—?"

"Don't touch me again. Ever. You're no longer a guest on this ranch. You just work here, like every other ranch hand before you."

Set back by her abrupt rejection, Raitt impatiently jammed his hat brim low over his forehead. "From what Dunc's told me, one of the cowhands didn't 'just work here.'"

"Budd was the only exception, and Granddad had no right to tell you anything personal about me." She whirled and headed blindly toward Lucille.

"Hold it!" Raitt commanded so sharply that she halted for a moment. "Besides not touching you, what other rules apply to my job?"

"Ranch hands sleep in the tack room. I'll have it clean and ready for you by tonight. The bunk is long and wide, and the stable bathroom works, shower and everything."

"What about meals?"

"I'll cook breakfast and dinner, and pack you a lunch to bring out here each day. This fence will take you several days to repost and wire."

"Just me? Not us working together?"

"I'll work alone on my own projects, Raitt." There was the stable roof to mend, for one thing. "Your days off are Saturday and Sunday. Your house privileges include the washer and dryer and TV in the evenings as late as you want."

"In other words," he concluded dryly, "you're the head honcho and I'm the hired help."

"In Granddad's absence, yes. Those are his standing rules for hired help."

Raitt mockingly tipped the brim of his hat. "Whatever you say, boss lady. I'll never unbutton you again, unless you personally ask me to do you the favor. If you ever ask, you'd better mean it."

Eager to escape the suggestive gleam in his eyes, Jessica skinned off her gloves to button up her shirt, then mounted Lucille.

"I'll leave this job to you, Raitt. Quitting time is yours to call—not too early, not too late."

"What time will breakfast and dinner be served?"

"Look for breakfast in the oven each morning. Same with dinner at night."

His jaw tightened. "After you've dined alone long enough, look for dessert in my bunk."

She reined Lucille around and rode off so fast that Marcus reared and shied out of her way.

9

RAITT DIDN'T consciously decide to woo Jess into changing her mind about his living arrangements. Charming her into reversing the rules was the last thing on his mind when he had to eat his first oven-warm dinner—a turkey pot pie—alone the first night. It wasn't on his mind when he went to bed mad, either.

The next morning, though, disliking his first oven-warm breakfast alone, he left a short note for Jess on the table.

We both stepped out of line yesterday, whatever our reasons. Let's be friends. Just friends. R.M.

He spotted her on the stable roof when he went out to saddle Cody. Leaving the lunch and water bottle she'd prepared for him at the base of the ladder, where Murph and Muttley had settled down, he advised them, "Don't even think about scarfing up my midday meal."

He climbed the ladder to the roof. Up top, he got an unobstructed view of Jess's firm, rounded bottom, wearing saddle-worn denims. *Very nice.*

Uncertain as to whether she had noticed him or was simply ignoring his ascent, he stopped on the last rung and cleared his throat. She skittered six inches down the slope before regaining a foothold.

"Sorry. Didn't mean to startle you."

"What do you want that can't wait?" she snapped.

"Dogs. Mind if I take Murph and Muttley with me today—for company?"

"Whatever they want to do is fine." She returned to pulling nails out of the roof with a claw hammer. "I don't need them today."

"I'll see you later, then." He stepped down a rung, but lingered there, looking at her.

"Well, go if you're going."

"I'm on my way," he assured her, though he was still busy, taking in the firm, rounded view. "You're up earlier than usual."

"The better to get a full day's work done. The horses —including Cody—are fed and watered. I put the others out, but left him in for you."

"Thanks. Stalls mucked out, too?"

She nodded. "Your job is the fence. Don't keep it waiting."

"You're the boss lady." He tipped his hat, savored the view one last time and went down the ladder.

Inside the stable he greeted his horse. "Whatcha think, pal? Not a bad place for your six-month vacation, huh? Other horses treating you better than the boss treats the hired help?"

Cody rubbed his nose affectionately on Raitt's sleeve, and Raitt scratched behind the gelding's ears.

"No street kids to make friends with here, I'm afraid. Yeah, I miss the luckless kids, too. Glad I don't have to miss you, as well."

Jessica peered at Raitt through the hole in the roof she was repairing. She saw him running his hands over the Appaloosa, checking out every bone and tendon. Her heart swelled. He and Cody obviously loved each other. She had the same deep love for her own horses, knew how emotionally fulfilling the relationship could be.

Raitt's concern for Cody was evident in the way he examined the animal. She checked her own the same way, every morning.

An image popped into her head of Raitt's hands moving over her own body in the same careful, caring way. She blinked to refocus on reality and saw that Raitt was looking in her direction, presumably because she had stopped making a noise.

"Jess?" he called. "Are you okay up there?"

"A-okay," she called back, and resumed ripping out nails and shingles.

He rode out on Cody a few minutes later, and she tried, in vain, not to watch. His broad shoulders. His muscled thighs. The low, cocky angle of the hat brim over his eyes. Murph and Muttley streaked ahead on the trail. Cody broke into a trot, heading after them. Suddenly she felt lonely again.

She didn't feel better until she took a midmorning break—and discovered that Raitt had gone off and left his lunch at the foot of the ladder.

RAITT CHECKED HIS WATCH when the sun rose past high noon. Would Jess ride out with his lunch? Would she guess that he'd purposely left it behind, or would she think it was a careless oversight on his part? Was she reading the note he'd left? Agreeing with it, or throwing darts at it?

His stomach rumbled. He began thinking that Jess might not care if a hired hand starved to death under the hot summer sun. She might figure he'd learn his lesson best if she didn't deliver the lunch pack. Maybe he'd better put his shirt on, ride back and beg a bite to eat before thirst and starvation leveled him.

He saw Cody raise his head from grazing and prick his ears forward. Snoozing in the shade of a pine tree a moment before, Murph and Muttley suddenly sprang onto all fours. They rushed down the trail together, tails wagging, yipping a welcome. He heard clip-clopping hooves and Jess's piercing dog whistle.

Lunch.

Jessica came to the fence line and saw Raitt aim a fresh post into a hole. Bare-chested, he had worked up a visible sweat. Training her eyes away from his rippling muscles, she saw that he had progressed much further with the fence repair than she had anticipated. He had sunk as many posts in a half day as she managed in a whole day.

However, he'd been remiss to leave behind his meal and water. He was looking at her as if he hadn't yet realized his foolishness. Wasn't he even thirsty after setting that much fence on a hot day?

She rode up to him, holding the lunch pack up for him to see. "Are all SFPD horse cops as forgetful as you?"

He looked surprised, then abashed. "I forgot my lunch? Hey, sorry about that."

"Don't forget it tomorrow," she grumbled, handing it over. "I won't pick up after you the next time."

"I appreciate the trouble you took, Jess." He shucked off his gloves and took the pack from her, grazing her fingers with his, looking into her eyes.

"Well, Speed needed exercising, anyway," she allowed.

He smiled disarmingly. "Care to join me?"

Shrugging, she secured her reins and swung out of the saddle. "Speed can use a breather, I guess. I've already eaten, though."

Raitt led the way to a tall pine and settled on a carpet of pine needles in the shade. She stayed on her feet, leaning one shoulder against the tree trunk, deciding to be candid.

"I saw your note, Raitt."

"And?" Water bottle poised an inch from his mouth, he waited for her reply.

"'Just friends' makes a certain amount of common sense, considering our situation."

"I'll drink to that."

Jessica watched his throat muscles work as he drained half the bottle in one long gulp. His chest hair was damp, and she wondered if he worked as hard in bed as he had in the field. Being "just friends" wouldn't be possible if she kept thinking like this, wondering how he would make love.

Like Budd, maybe. Wham-bam. Budd hadn't stuck around to say, "Thank you, ma'am."

Raitt bit into one of the thick, roast beef sandwiches she had made for him. A sensuous moan of appreciation followed. "Good God, that's *great*."

"Grandma Lizbeth's roast recipe. The secret is in the garlic-mustard marinade."

Even though the recipe wasn't her own, Jess felt a warm glow of pride. There was an irresistible charm in a man appreciating a woman's cooking.

He patted a spot on the ground. "Rest your saddle sores, friend. Tell me more about your grandmother."

Hesitant, she sat several inches from the spot he'd indicated. "She could do anything—cook, sew, ride the steepest trail, herd cattle, make Granddad the happiest man in the world."

"Go on." Raitt started a major assault on the second sandwich.

"She was . . . admirable. Never idle and endlessly interesting."

"I'd say that's an accurate description of her granddaughter, as well."

She vigorously disagreed. "Not for even one moment. I follow her recipes, rather than create my own, as she did. I can sew and quilt, but the fine embroidery she did on my poppy blouse is beyond me."

"You're a noticeably accomplished woman, Jess. Take credit and thank your new friend for noticing."

"Thank you," she mumbled. "My compliments to you for setting so many posts in record time."

"Thanks, even though I'll be sore as hell tonight," he said, flexing his shoulder muscles. "I work out at the department gym in the city, but not work like this."

"How did last week go?"

"Mostly as expected. I cleared everything out of my fridge, notified the condo management that I'd be gone, followed up on a few of my kids."

"What are they like?"

"Hard on the outside, but starving for attention inside. Down on themselves and everyone else. I'd get nowhere helping them without Cody to break the ice. People often don't realize how much community service an animal can do."

Jessica sifted pine needles through her fingers. "I've always thought of mounted patrols as having more style than substance. They always seem to be in tourist areas."

He nodded. "You might be thinking of the federal park police's Fisherman's Wharf-Embarcadero unit. My unit is city police, Golden Gate Park. Beyond the park, our beats extend to the zoo, Lake Merced,

Dolores Park and so on. At times we do crowd control."

"Do you arrest a lot of criminals on your beat?"

"More than you'd think. Arrests and citations kept us mounties tall in the saddle. We're a sad lot now, though. I played penny poker one night last week with my patrol pals. Pennies, because we're all on forced leave or taking rock-bottom pay cuts to do boring desk jobs."

"You wouldn't be sore as hell tonight if you'd taken a desk job."

He gave her an unfriendly look. "I'd rather be sore, okay? Even if you don't want me working out here. I'll earn every penny Dunc pays, believe me."

Looking at the neat row of fence posts he'd sunk, Jessica couldn't disbelieve him. Where he'd stopped work, Cody and Speed were nosing the fresh post, nibbling the tasty new wood.

"Hey, Speed," she called. "Stop munching."

"You, too, Cody," Raitt added, pitching them two apples from his lunch to divert them. "One for each of you."

"There goes dessert." Jess sighed, then remembered the remark he'd made yesterday. She got to her feet. "I've got to get going, too."

"Before you go, will I find dinner for one in the oven again tonight?"

Jess prodded a rock on the ground with the toe of her boot. "Granddad and I usually eat dinner on TV trays and watch whatever's on the tube. If you don't mind the evening news or summer reruns . . ."

"I don't mind catching the news at six." He winked and teased, "What's for dessert?"

"Bunk flambé, candied ego or cad sherbet," she said, unsuccessfully fighting a grin. "Take your pick."

He threw back his head and laughed. "I'd rather eat crow."

"If you want, use Granddad's room while he's gone."

"Gladly, Jess."

"Well, see you at six."

"It's a date."

Jessica didn't argue. Anyway, his words were only a figure of speech. She hadn't had a date in the last decade. Secretly pretending she had one each night wouldn't hurt.

He'd never know or guess how she really felt about him. She'd never let it show that she was falling in love with the hired hand.

RAITT FOUND SATISFACTION during the rest of the week in forging a friendship with Jess. Less satisfying was sleeping alone in Dunc's four-poster bed. His room was a respectable distance from hers, a span Raitt fantasized traveling every night and morning.

Invariably he woke with an erection and erotic ideas of showering with Jess. He could barely hear the water running so far away but, in his imagination, heard every drop fall and visualized what would happen if he stepped in with her. She would be wet and sleek and steamy...her eyes would turn the deepest green as he soaped her breasts....

The ache was so deep that he often considered returning to the city and a dreary desk job. At times he wished for Dunc and Vangie to return and relieve the worst of the tension. Jess both puzzled and perplexed him, but most of all, she appealed to him so much that being just friends wasn't enough.

Although solid, hard work had earned him her grudging respect and lowered her defenses during the week, he spent every day wanting more than that.

More. But nothing serious.

He started thinking he'd be better off with a few street kids up here to keep his mind off Jess. Hard work and fresh air could set a kid straight. The thought took root and grew.

FIVE DAYS after Dunc and Vangie had skipped out, Jessica made breakfast for herself and Raitt as usual.

On the surface, she had settled into a friendly daily routine with him. Beneath the surface, there was nothing routine about her thoughts and desires. They were erotic, turbulent and rife with passionate yearning.

"'Morning, Jess." Raitt came in with Murph and Muttley, poured himself a cup of coffee and sat down at the table. The dogs flopped at his feet.

"You're up early on your day off," she observed.

"Day off?" he repeated, looking surprised. "It's Saturday already?"

She nodded. "Most hired hands light out of here on Friday night and don't come back from town till Monday at sunup."

"What does the rancher do? Go fishing?"

"Sometimes."

"Dunc mentioned a good lake. It had a flower name."

"Morning Glory," she said; Raitt's eyes today were bluer than her favorite lake at its best.

He was wearing faded jeans and a white tank top that showed off his muscles to perfection. She turned to face the stove so her thoughts—and the flush on her face—wouldn't show. Thank heaven, the heat that was gathering between her thighs *couldn't* show.

"Maybe we could fish Morning Glory today, Jess."

"Hotcakes or eggs for breakfast?" she said, lighting a burner.

"If you don't want to go fishing with me, say so."

She removed eggs and pancake batter from the fridge. "I have a lot of other things to do."

"Such as what?"

"Such as . . ." Her mind went blank. The sharp, disappointed way he was looking at her, she couldn't think beyond breakfast. "Hotcakes or eggs, Raitt?"

"Both, dammit." He took up the morning paper and walled her out, muttering, "I knew I should've gone into town last night and looked up Betsy Newman."

Jessica gritted her teeth. So he hadn't forgotten Betsy since the town picnic.

"Phone her up," she challenged. "She won't turn down a chance to fish with you."

Raitt glowered at her over the top of the sports section. "Why are *you* turning me down?"

"Because I know I'm just the closest convenience." She slammed the frying pan and the griddle onto the stove. "You want to fish and you don't know the way to Morning Glory. I do. Very convenient. You don't have any fishing equipment. I do. Very con—"

"Say one more word against me or yourself, Jess, and I'll forget we've been friends." He half rose from his chair. "Betsy is the only 'convenience' I've met since I came here. I'm not that hard up yet. If I was, I'd be in town right now, in her wide-open bed."

"Why did you bring her up then?"

"You turned me down, Jess. Damned if I'm going to bow and thank you kindly for it! Hell, I can see why you live like an old maid and haven't had a date in ten years. Who'd dare to ask unless he wanted his head bitten off?"

Sudden tears stung Jess's eyes. *Old maid. Ten years.* The past decade seemed to be closing in on her, squeezing her into a corner she couldn't get out of. The stove in front of her blurred, then she heard her tears plop onto the hot griddle and start sizzling.

Raitt heard them, too, and saw her shudder as she suppressed a sob. He clamped his mouth shut, regretting what he'd said, and went to her before she could stumble blindly out of the kitchen.

Touching her shoulder, he murmured, "I'm sorry. I woke up on the wrong side of the saddle today."

Instinct told him that she was horrified to be showing her emotions like this. In that she was like the kids on the streets. He had learned from them that it was best to extend just a small human touch and to be receptive.

"Can I pour you a cup of coffee?"

She drew in a deep breath and got out a shaky, "Ye-es."

Raitt reached around her and turned off the stove burners, then handed her a paper towel. He poured the coffee and took the cup to the table.

"Come sit down, Jess. Breakfast can wait until we clear the air."

"This is totally stupid of me," she said, sliding into the chair he held out. "I never cry. Ask Granddad if you don't believe me."

He sat down across from her and gave her a small smile. "You never do a lot of things. Never cry, never think of yourself as good company. Look, I don't want to fish with Betsy. I want to fish with you."

"Half of the time you don't make sense, Raitt."

"About what?"

"Betsy is beautiful. She's blond and stacked."

He nodded. "And she knows it. You, on the other hand, don't have any idea of your own appeal.

Sometimes you remind me of Tim Waverly, one of my kids."

Rolling her eyes, she scoffed, "I remind you of a scruffy street kid. Very appealing."

"I didn't mean it that way." He paused. "Tim's been on my mind a lot, the past few days. I've been thinking...."

"What?"

"Well, you and Dunc have taken in wild horses and adopted them. How about giving a troubled, unwanted kid or two a few days of ranch life? Tim would love the riding and working. He might see that there's more to life than selling himself short. I'd absorb the extra expense for his room and board, of course."

With two charity cases in the stable, Jessica couldn't pretend that Raitt's suggestion struck an unsympathetic chord. She had to admit that his concern for his kids was making her fall that much more in love with him. He felt deeply about them, hadn't forgotten them.

"It's a fine idea, but Granddad would also have to approve." She looked at the phone. "Call him at Vangie's and ask."

Raitt picked up the phone, making a wry face. "They haven't answered all week when we called. Probably haven't crawled out of the bedroom." Looking dubious, he dialed Vangie's number. His eyebrows went up when someone answered.

"Dunc, you old rattlesnake. It's Raitt. Yeah. Fine. No, it's you I want to talk to first."

Jessica sipped her coffee, listening as Raitt explained why he'd called.

"I'm thinking of Tim Waverly coming up first. He's thirteen and living in a group home I found for him. Last week he was teetering on the edge of running with his old gang again. A few days up here might tip the balance the other way. Jess has no objections. What do you say?"

He held the receiver away from his ear for her to hear Dunc exclaim, "Yes! We can bring him with us when we head back up there next week."

"Thanks," Raitt said, "I'll have the group home investigate the legalities." He spoke briefly with Vangie and hung up.

"Good news," he crowed, reaching across the table to squeeze Jessica's hand. "Couple more phone calls and we'll have cause to celebrate."

Caught up by his enthusiasm, she wriggled in her chair and grinned. What a sunny, summer day it was all of a sudden! Raitt's excitement was infectious, making her forget that she'd been frying tears on the griddle ten minutes ago.

Suddenly she heard the thump-thump of Murph and Muttley wagging their tails under the table.

Jessica's heartbeat took up the same vibrant rhythm while Raitt made two quick, efficient calls. By the time he'd completed them, her heart was soaring with the exuberant hope that he and Patton Ranch would make a difference in Tim's life.

"Except for the details, we've got it made," he exulted, pulling her out of her chair and waltzing her around the kitchen. "Jump for joy, Jess!"

She whirled with him, dipping, swooping and laughing breathlessly. It was the giddiest waltz of her life. The only waltz she'd even danced. She was Cinderella, and Raitt was Prince Charming, and sunlit stardust seemed to be sparkling on every surface.

She twined her arms around his neck and he lifted her off her feet into a tight, happy hug. The imaginary waltz tempo slowed, and he held her close, cheek to cheek.

"Ohh," he breathed against her ear. "Miss Jess." His lips nipped her earlobe, moved down the side of her throat and back up, under her chin.

She felt dizzy, weightless, powerless to control the need to furrow the fingers of one hand in his thick, golden hair. "Raitt, Raitt," she murmured, then she was kissing him, sucking his eager tongue into her mouth, showing him the love she had hidden all week.

He lowered her slowly until her toes touched the floor. She felt his arousal all the way down, strong and rigid, hot and male. His tongue moved in her mouth, communicating a need that matched the melting heat between her thighs.

His hands slipped up and down her back, molding her against his chest, then arching her spine over his forearm so that he could have more of her.

"Don't stop us now," he whispered, touching his lips to the fabric of her shirt over her breasts. "Not this time."

"I won't," she heard herself shakily reply. "I—" She sucked in her breath and held it as his teeth grazed one nipple and then the other "—want you."

"Now?"

"Yes." *With all my heart.*

"No strings, Jess," he cautioned, backing her up to the table.

"I know." She flattened her palms against his chest and swept them up to his shoulders, holding on until he eased her onto the tabletop. She pulled him down with her, then discovered what it meant to be carried away by the moment, to be out of control.

She had no thought for where she was. Raitt was all she could see. His burning, blue gaze, broad chest and shoulders were everything in her world right now, all she needed. She hooked her fingers into the curved front of his undershirt and drew him down to her.

Braced over her on one elbow, kissing her mouth again, he unbuttoned her blouse and opened it. Arching into his kiss, into his caressing hand, Jessica invited his fingers to explore.

"So soft," he whispered, kneading her breast in his cupped palm, laving her nipple with his tongue. "And so hard."

He started sucking and her thighs parted. His hand slid down between them and rubbed. "Jess, you're so hot. So hot! For me, honey?"

"Yes . . . ah . . . ohh . . ."

His fingers lowered her zipper and slipped beneath her panties. He stroked and she gasped. He circled and she moaned. He kept on loving her until she uttered a high, helpless cry and climaxed.

"Lord, Jess." He gathered her into his arms when her pleasure was complete and her body began to grow limp. "You make me feel like a king. Where's the closest bed? Tell me . . . I can't think right now."

"My room," she managed to reply.

He carried her there, kissing her feverishly all the way. Placing her on her unmade bed, he tugged off her boots and jeans. It began to dawn on her what had happened in the kitchen; he'd barely touched her and she'd lost all control. He had seen her lose it, *watched* her lose it. Embarrassed now, she grasped the front halves of her shirt and started to squirm away from him.

Then he stood and stripped off his undershirt, peeled off his jeans and briefs, and what she saw stopped her short. She saw a man poised on the edge of losing his own control. His arousal arrowed straight up, and he stood as bold as a stallion eager to mate.

He removed a small packet from one pocket, then tossed the jeans aside. "I've been thinking ahead, Jess."

"Thank you," she whispered, her eyes drawn to his erection.

"Don't touch me there yet," he warned gently, joining her on the bed. "I couldn't give you more than two seconds right now."

She struggled for words. "But I already... on the table..."

"Yeah. You sure did." He grinned, loosening the clasp of her fingers on her shirt and baring the soft fullness. "There's more. Lots more." Kissing and sucking her nipples, he began again.

Unable to resist, she began to let down her guard again. Clenching her fingers in his golden hair, guiding his head from side to side, she gasped softly, "Harder. Harder."

Raitt didn't hold back. He had already anticipated that her passion would be vigorous and down-to-earth once she became aroused. She was a rancher who lived close to nature, a woman as strong, active and athletic in her own way as he was. Naturally she needed and wanted the impact of his strength. He wanted hers, as well.

He settled his hips between her thighs and used his teeth, nipping and tugging the rosy-brown peaks of her breasts, drawing more and more encouragement from her. He felt her moving under him, undulating, writhing, clamping her thigh muscles around his hips as if riding a horse.

To preserve control, he had to pull away and brace himself above her. Her hands slid down his torso and cradled him, measured him, gloved him. Looking into

her eyes, he sensed briefly that he'd never again experience a moment like it.

"Easy, Jess, please. I want it to be good for you."

She stroked forward slowly to his flared tip, then
helped him put on a condom. "Raitt, take my panties
off. Hurry."

Straightening, he hooked his thumbs into the elastic and drew them off. Slowly. He needed some moments away from her touch, had a masculine need to
feast his eyes on the feminine wonders of her body.

"I want you to come again, honey," he murmured,
drawing one fingertip from the shallow dip of her na-
vel to the curly, dark nest farther down. "I want to do
it for you." He touched her pink folds, finding the
swollen, hidden bud within. "Tell me you want it,
too."

"I want . . . you inside me."

"After this," he promised, bending to kiss her dark,
glistening curls and taste her moist heat. He heard her
suck in her breath and hold it as his tongue focused on
her most sensitive spot.

Jessica had only imagined the ultimate kiss until
now. Budd hadn't done this. He hadn't done anything like what Raitt had done, was doing. Oh, this
was molten pleasure, far beyond anything she had
imagined. She began to pant and whimper—to fall
completely in love with Raitt Marlow.

"Now," she heard herself pleading brokenly. She
dug her nails into his shoulders. "Now—oh—
please . . . —"

"Wait for me," he rasped, kissing his way up her body to her breasts. "Take me in."

She only had to part her thighs a little more and he was there, his hardness penetrating, filling her. Braced on his forearms, he was kissing her closed eyelids, kissing her mouth, sharing the natural scent and flavor of her own body with her.

"Open your eyes, Jess. Look at me. Let yourself go again."

She opened them, met his gaze and wrapped her legs around him. She felt him begin to move in a slow, deep, thrusting rhythm. Everything intensified. Rippling and shuddering, she rode each long thrust to the highest peak.

A scream sounded; it was hers. A spasm of hoarse shouts followed, his. She went limp and he collapsed on top of her, burying his face in her hair.

Replete, glowing, Jessica held Raitt within her body and within her arms. She pretended that she was beautiful and that her prince loved her, even though she knew she wasn't and he didn't.

That would matter soon enough, but not this soon. Not yet.

10

JESSICA DIDN'T EMERGE from her bedroom until early afternoon. She dressed quietly, left Raitt asleep in her bed amid the tangled bedclothes, and left a note for him on the kitchen table.

Gone to town to stay with a sick friend. Spending two nights.

Taking a few necessities with her, she got into Dunc's pickup and left the ranch. After making love with Raitt all morning, she had to get farther away from him than a walk or a horseback ride could take her. She wouldn't be able to sit on a horse, anyway, for Raitt had been a strong, vigorous lover—and so had she.

She left, hoping to regain what she had begun to fear she had lost in bed with Raitt. Her independence. Her self-control. She wanted to call back the woman she had been before she met him, the one who didn't need a man.

Never mind what she had gained—more sexual experience and self-knowledge in one morning than in her entire life. She had even been shocked to discover that she was a screamer. To her greater surprise, Raitt had *loved* it. He had dedicated himself to inciting multiple screams. She hadn't known her capacity was so enormous.

He had taught her how to nurture his own response, too, and she had taken to the task with delight.

Steering the truck toward town, Jessica willed herself to remember that Raitt's stay at the ranch was temporary. He'd go back to his mounted unit in a few months, and she'd be left with a broken heart. Raitt wouldn't break it with the callousness that Budd had, but he'd leave, all the same.

No strings. Raitt had his reasons, and he'd made his intentions clear from the start.

RAITT SLOWLY AWOKE and reached for Jess. Realizing he was alone in her bed, he opened his eyes and called her name. No answer. The house was silent.

"Jess?"

His second call brought Murph and Muttley, scratching and whining at the closed bedroom door. Raitt found that odd. If Jess was nearby, the dogs would be with her.

Sitting up in bed, he stretched and found his muscles pleasantly sore. For good reason. Smiling smugly, he scratched his chest. What a day off! He'd never had one as good as this. He checked out the crease of his thigh, where Jess's suckling had left a mark. Still there. He arched around to see the other one she'd made on his right bun. Still there.

"Jess?" he called at the top of his lungs. The only answer was Murph and Muttley outside the door.

Raitt got up gingerly, pulled on his jeans and let the dogs in. "Where is she?"

They just wagged their tails and grinned expectantly. Realizing how starved he was, he padded barefoot into the kitchen and immediately saw the note.

He swore as he read it, then balled it in one hand. Since when did Jess have a sick friend in town? No phone number. No address. Like hell she had sick duty for the next two nights!

She was worse than a yo-yo, that woman. Reeling out in all her glory, then winding up tight in all her pride. And Raitt was damn sure it was her prickly pride that caused these unpredictable retreats into herself.

He flung himself into a chair and drummed his fingers upon the table, brooding; maybe he should have controlled himself after the first kiss. He stared at the tabletop, the scene of her initial orgasm.

In the kitchen, for Pete's sake! For sure, he could have shown more finesse than taking her to the moon on a breakfast table. Hadn't he learned over the years that every woman wanted to be romanced? It began to seem as if the only thing he'd done right was to satisfy her sexually—more often than he could count.

That had apparently not been enough. Women wanted romance. Even more, they wanted love.

And now, dammit, he was very close to feeling as if he loved her! That wasn't good, he admitted; something deeper than lust had expressed itself in her bed. Love. He could hardly believe it.

Maybe it wasn't the L-word, he reasoned. Maybe he was just weakened by more sex than he'd ever had at one time. Maybe he'd better phone Dunc and find out where the hell Jess could have gone.

"Ten to one she's holed up at the old homestead cabin on the east slope," Dunc said when Raitt called and read him the note. "She goes there to unruffle her feathers. You been rufflin' 'em?"

"Something like that," Raitt muttered, then deepened his tone to a menacing level. "How are you treating my grandmother, by the way?"

"Keepin' a special smile on the lady's face, boy."

Raitt scowled helplessly. "Just out of curiosity, how would I find that cabin if I wanted to spend a day off there?"

"Well, first you head toward town. Halfway to town, take a little dirt road you'll see off to your left."

Dunc continued to give directions and Raitt wrote them down, a complex maze of numbered, unpaved fire roads.

"The last stretch of road's rutted pretty deep," the older man advised. "Take it careful in that hot rod of yours. The footpath to the cabin's overgrown, too. You headin' up there to look for Jessie?"

"Hell, no! I'm the hired hand, not her keeper."

"She needs both," Dunc grumbled.

"Dunc, while you're in San Francisco, do me one big personal favor, will you?"

"Sure as shootin'. What?"

"Put a stop to the special smile on my grandmother's face."

HOLED UP in the snug, one-room cabin on her second night away from the ranch, Jessica poked listlessly at the fire she had lighted in the potbellied stove.

She hadn't been able to stop brooding, reliving Raitt's kisses and caresses, trying to regret all that had happened. She hadn't been able to stop worrying, either—about the ranch, the horses and the chores she had dumped into Raitt's hands on his two days off. How would she explain that much overtime pay to Granddad?

What could she possibly say to Raitt when she returned? What if he refused the order she intended to give him to move out of the house and back into the tack room? Shaking her head, she put out the fire for the night and changed into a long nightshirt.

Last night she hadn't slept well. First, a bear had come snuffling around the cabin at midnight. She had beaten a saucepan with a spoon to scare the animal and it had fled, crashing through the trees and brush. Soon after, a coyote had begun howling in the distance. The plaintive cry had gone on and on, making her wish for Raitt's strong arms around her.

It was the first time she had ever felt lonely at the cabin. The place had always been a welcoming refuge before, simply furnished and well stocked with canned food. A nearby spring provided clear, mountain water. What more could a woman want—besides the man she loved?

Cursing the direction of her thoughts, she made sure the saucepan and spoon were handy, turned off the gas lantern and got into bed. It was odd, but the mattress had never seemed lumpy until now, nor had the flannel sheets and quilt provided so little warmth.

She twisted and turned, then heard a twig crack outside. Sighing, she took up the pan and spoon, made a racket, then stopped and listened for sounds of the frightened bear bounding away.

Instead it grunted and clawed at the log door.

Jessica's heart bolted into her throat. The animal was acting rabid. She drummed up a noise so deafening that her ears rang when she stopped and listened again.

The door burst open. Screaming, she leaped out of bed and sprang for the wood ax by the fireplace.

Huge and snarling, a dark shape lumbered through the doorway. Jessica screamed louder and raised the ax.

"Dammit," the shape growled. "It's only me."

"R-R-Raitt?" She dropped the ax with a clatter.

"Damn flashlight burned out," he groaned. "Damn stinging nettles everywhere. I don't need any of this."

"What are you doing here?"

"Dying a slow death," he moaned. "For God's sake, turn on a light."

She lurched to the table where the lantern and matches were. The first match broke on the striker. The second flared into flame, illuminating Raitt's face as she shakily lighted the lantern. His features were twisted with pain. He was wearing a sheepskin cattleman's jacket and holding his hands outstretched in front of him.

"Raitt, what's wrong?"

"I fell hands down into a nettle patch when my flashlight blew." He slumped into a chair at the table. "Pick out the stickers. Hurry!"

"Yes. Right away." She rushed to the first aid kit and brought it to the table. "Here's some sunburn-pain spray and a pair of tweezers." She pulled out the spray and shook the can. "Hold still."

He shut his eyes and clenched his jaw while she sprayed both hands. Then, as the topical anesthetic brought quick relief, he let out a sigh.

"Better?"

"Much better. Why is there a blasted nettle patch blocking the footpath out there?"

Tweezing carefully, she started to take out the stinging barbs. "There's a side path around it. I was going to clear the patch out tomorrow."

"A little too late, Jess."

Pressing her lips together, wishing he didn't sound so accusing, she worked on his hands in silence. He didn't say any more, either, just watched what she was doing. Finally every stinger had been plucked out.

He flexed his palms and fingers. "Human again."

"It would have been worse if you didn't have work calluses," she observed. "Stay still again and I'll rub some antiseptic on for you." She opened a tube of gel and began to spread the medicine in circles upon one palm.

"That feels good." He watched her slim, deft fingers smoothing the clear mixture on his broad palm. She had touched the nipples on his chest the same way the other morning. "Real good," he added huskily.

"How did you find me?" she asked, her own voice sounding throaty and sexy.

"Dunc. He seemed to know you'd be here. I didn't believe your note for a minute."

"Oh." She continued stroking the gel from his palms to his fingers, her movements slowing as she reached the tips. Any slower and it would be an outright caress, he thought.

More and more slowly she circled, her eyes tracking the erotic motion.

"*So* good," he encouraged, feeling himself grow hard. *So* hard.

He watched Jess's dark lashes sweep long shadows over her cheeks in the lantern light. Her glossy hair reflected the glow. Her lips were parting. The tip of her tongue was moistening them. She switched to the other hand and spread more gel—still more slowly.

"Jess?"

"Hmm?"

Curling his fingers around hers, he cradled her hand. She looked up, he leaned forward and kissed her moistened lips.

"Let's go to bed," he murmured. "I've had a hell of a day. I need you."

He rose, drawing her out of the chair and into his arms, holding her so that she could feel the passion her touch had aroused.

"Need me, too, Jess."

Out in the night, a coyote began to howl. Farther away, another coyote made it a duet. Low on gas, the lantern flickered and dimmed.

Raitt felt Jess hesitate, then move fully into his embrace. "I shouldn't," he heard her whisper. "I really shouldn't."

She was, however, freeing the top button of his shirt as she whispered those words, so he shrugged off his heavy shearling and let it fall to the floor. Gathering her up once more, he kissed her long and deep and reveled in the unique flavor of her mouth. The need to possess her speared through him, sharply, urgently, making him coil his muscles and quiver.

He could feel that she wore nothing under her nightshirt. Cut high at the sides, it reached the middle of her thighs. Slipping his hands under it, he cupped her bare buttocks and lifted her against him. He felt her legs wrapping around his waist, her soft core molding against his aching hardness, her tongue stroking his own.

He had hoped to be gentle and tender, yet wild and primitive urges made him want her to ride his body. She was clinging tightly, making passionate sounds in the depths of her throat. Then she bowed her spine, offering her breasts to him, and he was kissing them, licking them, wetting the fine cotton that stretched over the stiff points of her nipples.

"Unzip," she panted, gripping his shoulders and grinding the center of her body against him. "I can't wait . . . can't wait. . . ."

He took a condom from his pocket and undid his belt, then let her unzip his jeans and sheath him in protection. "Take me with you," he rasped, thrusting into her to the hilt. "Ride me hard."

She set a frantic, desperate pace that stampeded his senses. With one hand he ripped open the front of her nightshirt. Buttons went flying, and she made a throaty sound of approval and encouragement. He closed his lips over one nipple and sucked hard, the way he knew she liked it.

"Yess," he heard her hiss. Her fingers drove into his hair, she shuddered, then screamed. Not the way she had screamed when he burst the door open. Not the way she had when she'd reached for the ax.

A high, clear, pulsing sound, it was a siren song that summoned him to his final, deep upsurge.

"Yes!" He reached hot, wild completion.

Gasping hoarsely, he reeled under the impact of the ecstasy they had shared. Moving two steps to one of the chairs, he sank into it to preserve their union and savor the afterglow.

She wilted against him. "My God, Raitt!"

He nodded, nuzzling the soft curves of her breasts. "This is heaven, all right."

More of heaven than he'd ever known with a woman, he thought. He had come here, craving another taste of paradise with Jess, and she had given it to him without reserve. He hadn't been able to stay away. Two days had been too long to wait. Even the idea that he might be falling in love hadn't stopped him.

He recalled that he had been halfway in love once or twice before and had been able to handle it. Friendship had been possible after the end. He'd do the same with Jess, he promised himself.

But how could a man think clearly with paradise straddling his hips? Parting her nightshirt, he mouthed cherishing kisses over her heart. He felt it skip a beat—for him.

"Are you comfortable, Miss Jess?"

"Yes."

"Me, too." So comfortable that he soon thickened inside her and began moving again. Slowly, tenderly this time, gently, searchingly, touching his fingers to the swollen bud between her legs as he moved within her, wanting everything for her and from her. But *for* her, first.

Love. He could handle it if he was careful.

The lantern went dark. Outside, the coyotes stopped howling. Inside, there were only the sounds of two lovers' sighs.

RAITT WOKE WITH A START at dawn, hearing something pant and grunt outside the window by the bed.

He peered out and blinked at what he saw—a big, dark brown bear, warily inspecting a woodpile. Swallowing hard, Raitt nudged Jess.

"We've got a bear for company."

"Beat the pan with the spoon," she mumbled sleepily.

He remembered her doing that last night and deafening him. Then she had almost axed him. Looking at the bear out there, he could see why.

It was beautiful in a "Wild Kingdom" sort of way, but he'd rather be observing a mugger or a car thief in the backyard. He had efficiently dealt with plenty of those in San Francisco. He'd never dealt with one of these, anywhere.

The pan and spoon on the bed stand looked like a paltry defense, incapable of putting fear into anything.

"Beat it like a drum," Jessica mumbled. "He'll run away."

Raitt reached for his tools. "Promise?"

"Promise." She yawned and covered her ears.

He banged the spoon against the pan and discovered that Jess was right. The bear wheeled and sped away, churning through the underbrush.

"Jeez, it's fast on its feet," he marveled. "Noisy, too." It was out of sight, but could still be heard, crashing through the woods.

Relieved, Raitt settled down again with Jess and rumpled her hair. It slipped through his fingers like dark silk. He combed it and watched it fall into a soft, crescent shape on her pillow.

"Good morning, sleepyhead." He waited for her eyes to open. Sage green, they'd turn dark emerald if he started caressing her. They'd deepen almost to black at the moment of her climax. He had missed watching them do so last night.

After a night like that, his body was spent, but he suspected that hers might not be. He knew he didn't need an erection to fulfill her needs. That was what she preferred, of course, and it made him feel on top of the world every time she praised his virile strength.

Still, she loved other options, too, and so did he. Never had he felt so fortunate, so well matched. He took great care to remind himself that *matched* and *mated* were two different things.

Gazing at Jess and anticipating what pleasure he could offer her was probably not the smartest thing to be doing right now. Especially since spending the night with her seemed to have drawn some of his deeper emotions too close to the surface. He shouldn't be thinking how superior loving Jess was, compared to having friendly, manageable sex.

He had to force himself not to do more than twine her hair around his thumb and watch her wake up.

Jessica opened her eyes and returned Raitt's steady gaze. That wasn't love she saw in his eyes, she cautioned herself. It was smug, male satisfaction in knowing that he was sexually irresistible to her. After last night, his ego couldn't have one single doubt.

"What do you have here for my breakfast, Miss Jess?" He trailed his fingers from her hair to her breast.

Exerting an enormous effort to reject what he obviously had in mind, she sat up and turned her bare back to him.

"Early chores have to be done at the ranch, Raitt. We'd better get going."

He smoothed his open hand down her spine and sighed. "You're the boss. I'm only the hired hand whose two days off are over too soon."

"I'm sorry I left you responsible for everything during your time off," she said, plucking her nightshirt from the cabin floor. The torn front reminded her of how much she had allowed to happen. She could have stopped Raitt, yet hadn't put up even a token resistance. She had abandoned herself to him. Again.

Rising from the bed, she went to the front window and looked out. Sunrise tipped the highest visible mountain peaks with a buttery-gold light.

"I shouldn't have come up here. You shouldn't have, either, Raitt."

"I almost didn't get here at all, Jess. Dunc's directions didn't sound as complicated as they turned out to be. Who's in charge of keeping the number signs on the fire roads up here, anyway? Half of them aren't signed."

She shrugged. "It's easy to get lost if you don't know the way."

"I got major lost," he admitted. "Then my flashlight burned out on the path. All for you." His tone changed, hardened. "Why did you run out on me?"

"How was Granddad when you phoned him?"

"Turn around, look me in the eye and answer me, Jess. You ran out. Why?"

She turned, determined to be honest. "Because I could love you. It's too much to get over when you go back to the city."

"*Could* love me? But don't?" He threw back the quilt, got out of bed and pulled on his jeans. "Or just plain won't?"

"Can't. I have independence here, more than most women can claim. Depending on you for love or anything else right now would be . . ." She turned back to the view. "You aren't even a marrying man."

"Love and marriage are two different things," he countered, buttoning his shirt. "We could do love without marriage. I could handle that with you."

Raitt was surprising himself with those words. He wasn't certain when he'd decided that love could be within his comfort zone. Maybe right now. He was damned glad to be with Jess, despite the hellish trip to the cabin.

"I'm not foolish enough to believe you love me, Raitt. Men have never pursued me, even idly—except Budd, for his personal body count and a beer-bar bet."

"Bet?"

"A big bet." She glanced defiantly over her shoulder. "I was the plainest, oldest virgin in these parts at the time. Bored cowpunks will place bets on just about anything when they get liquored up at the town tavern."

"What happened, exactly?"

"Somebody bet Budd that he couldn't seduce me. Budd decided he could use the bucks to pay off some heavy gambling debts and skip town. Later I heard that he had put a tape recorder under his bed to get the proof he needed to win."

"That bastard!" Raitt spat out the words.

Jessica directed a grim, bitter smile at the sun-tipped peaks. "He swore that he loved me. I believed every word."

"Jess, I'm not feeding you a line. I wasn't waging a bet when I paid big to picnic with you. Something about you got to me, even then. It really got to me the other morning, in bed with you."

"The other morning happened because you're a male and I'm a female with no one else but each other within miles and miles," she said, finding her own jeans and stepping into them. "Last night was more of the same antidote to loneliness and isolation."

"Jess," he said roughly, grasping her arm and making her look at him. "You left me a flat-out lie in your note, so I came here looking for the truth. I wanted an apology, too. Maybe I was even looking for some sort of hope that . . ." He paused, unable to explain to her, or to himself, his reasons for being here.

She freed herself from his grasp. "Hope of what? Not anything lasting. We both know where you stand on that, don't we?"

"I made everything clear to you at the beginning," he retorted defensively, tugging on his boots. "And now I'm beginning to wonder what I see in you that I never see elsewhere. Maybe you're not as gorgeous inside as I was starting to think."

"Don't give me that old crock," she scoffed. "Budd used the same, sappy 'inner beauty' line already. It only works once with me."

Raitt threw up his hands. "You're hopeless."

"Why would I hope for anything but supercharged sex from a man who's scared spitless and spineless?"

"Of what?"

"Love, marriage and lifelong commitment!"

He swiped his shearling jacket from the floor. "Get yourself back to the ranch in time for evening chores, because I won't be there to do that or anything else anymore. The most boring desk job has to be better than wrangling day and night with you."

"Where shall I send your paycheck?" she inquired icily.

"Apply it to Cody's room and board until I find out what to do with him." He stomped through the door and slammed it shut.

Jessica's eyes smarted with tears. She clenched her jaw and told herself her heart wasn't broken enough to cry over. Raitt would have had to leave sooner or later. Sooner was better by far. After a few, back-breaking days of keeping the ranch on track by herself, the memory of him would begin to fade.

Soon he'd be pushed to the outer limits of her mind, where Butt Cockroach had been withering away for ten years. Ratt Marshmallow would be good company for Butt.

She sat down at the table and sobbed into her hands.

11

JESSICA LEFT THE CABIN and drove to town. She wanted to give Raitt time to pack up and clear out, and needed to see another human face besides his. She'd pass some time at the Feed-and-Tack and restore her inner balance.

Pete, the store owner, was one of Dunc's old cronies. He kept a big barrel of peanuts for his customers and a circle of old chairs around the barrel. Folk were always welcome to shoot the breeze and litter the floor with peanut shells.

"Hey, Gimpy," Pete said when she walked in. Stooped by rheumatism and genial by nature, without anyone else in the store at the moment, he rocked back in his chair at the peanut barrel and invited her to take a seat. "How's the bum ankle you had at the picnic?"

"All well, Pete." She rotated it to show him.

"How's Dunc? Haven't seen much of the old geezer since Vangie came to visit him."

"He's visiting *her* in San Francisco now."

Pete smiled approvingly. "They looked to me like a good match at the picnic. You don't look too happy about the situation, though."

"I've caught an allergy of some sort," she fibbed, cracking a peanut, aware that her eyes were still red-rimmed. *An allergic reaction to Raitt Marlow.*

"Doc Coulter says Dunc took Vangie's grandson on as a hired hand."

She shrugged. "He quit the job today. Couldn't seem to cut it."

"No?" Pete cracked a shell and popped the nuts into his mouth. "The whole town's still jabbering about what he paid for your picnic basket. He looked to me like he had all the right stuff, and then some."

"It turned out to be the wrong stuff. He's on his way back to the city by now."

Pete frowned. "I thought I saw that red-hot car of his drive by a bit earlier." Suddenly bleary-eyed, he shook his head. "Guess not. When is Dunc coming back?"

"Soon, I hope." She rocked back in her own chair and tried to enjoy another peanut. "What's been happening around here since the picnic?"

"You haven't heard?" His eyes grew round and his hunched spine almost straightened.

"Heard what?"

"Budd Cochran's back in town."

She almost tumbled backward. "Where?"

"Over at the tavern, right this second. Playing poker."

Right that second, she was wholeheartedly grateful to Ratt Marshmallow for enabling her to cover her shock and dismay, arch an eyebrow and scoff, "The one, the only Butt Cockroach?"

Pete burst into laughter. "Butt!" he hooted, hanging on to the barrel to keep from rolling on the floor. "Cockroach!"

"Put in an extra supply of roach spray, Pete," she suggested jauntily, getting up and sauntering out the door as if Budd's return was of no concern to her.

Outside, her first thought was to jump into the truck and head back home as fast as the truck would go. If Budd was the latest news in town, people would be remembering the bet he'd made and won ten years ago. She, the focus of that bet, couldn't walk down the street right now. It was bad enough that she had walked into Pete's store without knowing what must have entered his mind when he saw her.

Not that Pete or anyone had been mean back then. They hadn't. But they had gossiped as people do, and her greatest personal humiliation had become public knowledge overnight. She had been living it down—and living on chin-up pride—ever since.

Oh, how she'd love to get her hands on that cowpunk and strangle him! Even before she reached the truck, wrapping her fingers around his neck started to seem like the best idea she'd ever had. She found herself turning around and marching straight toward the tavern.

Halfway there, she saw Betsy Newman bouncing toward her.

"Jessie, hi."

Jessica didn't stop. "I can't talk now, Betsy."

Betsy turned and caught up with her. "What's wrong?"

"Nothing that strangling a certain low-down cow-punk won't fix."

"Budd, you mean?"

"Who else would I mean?"

"What are you going to do?"

"Just choke him until he gags for mercy. That's all."

"Oh, my God." Betsy gleefully clapped her hands. "Don't do it until I round up an audience for you."

Betsy sprinted off in the opposite direction and Jessica marched on down Main Street without a mis-step. She felt like the sheriff in "High Noon," but not half as apprehensive. She was fed up to the end of her ponytail with hired hands.

She barged through the tavern door and stepped inside, glaring. A hush fell over the bar. It was noon and the place was almost full.

She spotted him at the poker table in the corner. He had his back to her, but she'd know him anywhere. He was still a punk, hat cocked on the back of his head, worn-down boot heels hooked in the rungs of his chair. His black cowboy shirt should have had a white fur stripe down the middle. His hair was scrag-glier, but still cow-cookie brown.

"Well, danged if it isn't Butt Cockroach back there," she drawled loudly, advancing through the tavern.

He turned in his chair and blanched.

Cal, the beefy tavern owner, chuckled behind the bar. "Butt?" he echoed, then broke into a braying guffaw.

Everyone else along the bar joined him laughing, and she mentally thanked Raitt again. Someone even added a shoot-em-up rodeo whistle to the response.

It encouraged her to take a full beer bottle out of someone's hand as she passed, and to swagger right up to the poker table.

"Mr. Cockroach. Ten years, no see." What a pleasure to make the insect squirm. He looked shocked, speechless and as if drained of all his blood. "I guess you didn't expect me to walk right in here and tell you just what you are, did you—*Butt?*"

"No buts about it," snickered someone at the bar.

She regarded the three other poker players. "What are you playing, boys? Stud poker? You three seem to be the only studs present at this table."

She watched smugly as his partners started fingering their hats and edging their chairs away from the table. Glancing at Budd, she noticed his mouth begin to close. He appeared to be regaining at least one of his precious few faculties.

"Jessie," he croaked.

She nodded. "Me, Butt. Won any good bets lately?"

"Yeah, Butt," someone called out. "Wanna wager you'll get outta Cal's place alive?"

"Don't bet on it," she advised him, wondering what on earth to do now that she had him cornered and everyone rooting for her. Had she never noticed before how close to scrawny his build was? Had his eyes always been a dull, washed-out gray? Compared to Raitt, he was a lackluster miniature of a male.

"Jessie," he croaked again, helplessly gesturing with his handful of poker cards.

"Aren't some of your cards supposed to match in poker?" she inquired innocently. "Yours aren't doing that. Even the little heart and the diamond and the spade don't match with anything else you're holding."

Hearing that, one stud checked his own cards with new eyes. "Trying to bluff me, huh, partner?"

"Can I—" Budd paused to swallow "—buy you a beer, Jessie?"

"Take a big hint from the one I've already got." She flicked off his hat and poured the beer over his head.

He backed up his chair, blinking and sputtering, and someone handed her another full bottle over her shoulder.

"Have another," she offered sweetly, upending that one over him, too.

A third bottle arrived and she took hold of it. The hand providing it didn't let go, however. She tugged, then turned and found herself looking into a pair of morning-glory-blue eyes.

"Raitt!"

Budd surged out of his chair, swearing, one fist lashing out. Jessica ducked the punch, and Raitt caught it in a steely, midair grip.

Jessica watched him twist Budd's wrist so fast and hard that Budd howled in pain and buckled at the knees.

"If you're smart, Butt, you'll thank Miss Jess for the two beers she bought you," Raitt said, still twisting and forcing him down. "That's a good boy. On your knees."

Clawing ineffectually at Raitt with his free hand, Budd gritted his teeth. "You bastard."

"Thank her nicely, now." Raitt cranked up the pain level.

Budd howled like a coyote. "Thank you, Jessie."

"Encore," one of the bar patrons demanded.

"Thank you, Jessie."

"Once more for good measure," Jessica insisted quickly, pouring the third beer over his head.

"ThankyouJessie."

She met her ally's steady blue gaze as he released Budd. "Thank you, Raitt."

He tipped his hat. "No problem, Miss Jess."

Budd staggered to his feet and elbowed his way through the circle of onlookers, hissing a string of bitter cuss words all the way out the door.

Jessica saw now that the tavern was packed. Everyone in town had apparently come running to witness the showdown. Pete and Betsy. Doc Coulter and his office receptionist. Betsy's truck mechanic. The postmaster and two grocery clerks. The gas station crew.

They all crowded close, shaking her hand, slapping Raitt on the back.

"I got it all on tape!" Betsy crowed, brandishing a camcorder. "Color, sound, the whole enchilada."

"The next round of drinks is on the house," Cal declared magnanimously. Cheering his generosity, the crowd shifted and mobbed the bar.

Jessica looked again at Raitt. "What are you doing in town?"

"Gassing up my car and changing the oil before driving to San Francisco. Betsy raced by, spreading the word, and I followed the crowd."

"You were . . . wonderful."

He shrugged. "He deserved to pay in full for what he did to you. You were doing just fine, but I wanted to see him really crawl."

"I could never have muscled him to his knees like you did."

"What you were doing was the equivalent of it, Jess. He couldn't have walked out of here with much dignity after you poured the first beer." He gave her a twisted half grin. "Butt Cockroach. Glad I thought of it."

"I don't know how to thank you."

His smile faded out. "Yes, you do. Change your mind about us."

"My feelings about commitment and marriage will never change, Raitt. They're fundamental."

"Mine are fundamental, too," he countered. "If you'd loosen up on the marriage-commitment angle—"

"No," she said firmly.

"—we could stay friends for the next six months."

"We're much more than friends, Raitt." Her fingers started itching for a six-pack to pour over him.

"I'm on my way, then."

"Good. Don't be at the ranch when I get back."

"Trust me, Jess, I'll be long gone."

She turned her back, refusing to cry one more tear, refusing to watch him walk through the door and out of her life.

He had gone from Ratt to Raitt and then back to Ratt again. She was through with him.

As PROMISED, he'd packed up and gone when Jessica returned to the ranch. She struggled to feel relieved, but dejection crowded out what little relief she felt.

Even Teardrop seemed to be feeling the same way when Jessica fed and watered her that evening. Alamo, on the other hand, was feistier than ever, seeming to sense that the competition was history. He was king stud again, making a big physical show of his status.

Jessica immediately started thinking about getting him a jockstrap. The last thing she needed was a graphic reminder of Raitt Marlow every day.

Cody, however, was the most powerful reminder. Raitt's horse led her thoughts to the man's inner qualities. She'd had to admire his expert horsemanship and concern for kids like Tim Waverly. His actions in the tavern had been both brave and honorable, as well as physically daunting. He had put Budd down more effectively than she could ever have done without his help.

Tim wouldn't be coming to the ranch now, and Raitt must be regretting that. She found herself disappointed, too. She had looked forward to meeting the boy.

The phone rang that night and Jessica caught her breath, thinking Raitt might be the caller. Her palms dampened and her heartbeat started to gallop. She touched the phone and it seemed to sizzle with energy. Picking it up, she could hardly speak.

"Hello?"

"Howdy, gal. Looks like you chased Raitt off so's he'll never have nothin' more to do with you or my ranch. You crazy, or what?"

"I didn't chase him off. He chose to go—a wise decision, all things considered."

Dunc snorted. "Wise, huh? Never heard a dumber thing in my whole life than when he called to say he'd moved back. I don't like the idea of you bein' alone up there."

"I don't need Ratt, period."

"Ratt?" he growled. "Was he a varmint toward you, gal? Makin' empty promises, settin' up your expectations?"

"No, but he's a rat, nonetheless."

"If he set you up for hurt, Jessie, I'll make him real sorry for it."

"He didn't, Granddad, honestly. Did you call for any reason other than to bawl me out?"

"Yep. Got an earthshakin' announcement to make. Vangie and I are gettin' married. We're tyin' the knot over in Reno this comin' Saturday."

Jessica blinked. "Married? Reno?"

"Reno's more fun than the big city. More Western atmosphere there to suit two ex-Texans."

"But you've known Vangie less than—"

"The heart knows, gal. Doc Coulter's flyin' to Reno to be best man. You're a bridesmaid and Raitt's an usher. Should be fun to watch the both of you walk down the same aisle."

"It's not a joke. I have personal reasons for thinking of him as Ratt, Granddad."

"And I'm in no mood to argue with a herd of mules," Dunc warned. "Where's the congratulations I should be gettin'? Your folks and your sister are all smiles about addin' another member to the family. They'll be here early to cheer us on."

Jessica sighed. "I'm sorry, Granddad. Of course I'll be there." She put her best effort into sounding happy for him. "Congratulations. It couldn't happen to a nicer couple."

"That's the Jessie I know and love," he said approvingly. "Now, you find somebody to tend the chores while you're here. Get a frilly dress, too, and curl your hair up pretty. Make a nice impression on

Vangie's clan, like I did. Drive the truck down. Here's the address."

Jessica wrote down the details he gave her. Everyone in the wedding party would be transported from San Francisco to Reno in a deluxe, chartered bus. All the arrangements were in place. Her presence was expected at a Marlow-Patton dinner for family and friends on Friday evening.

She had four days to find a frilly dress and adjust her attitude toward walking down the aisle with her grandfather's ex-hired hand.

THE DAY AFTER Dunc's call, Jessica drove his pickup to town. The weather was unusual, muggy and overcast, unsettled. Dunc would have called it a "freak thunder and lightnin'" day. As usual during the summer, the weather report on the truck radio advised listeners of the current fire-danger level. High today.

Jessica didn't pay strict attention. She was too preoccupied with memories of Raitt—and the disagreeable idea of shopping for a dress and hair curlers. There were two clothing stores and one variety store in town. Since she only felt comfortable at the Feed-and-Tack, she went over there first.

Pete grinned when she walked in. "Guess who got his butt out of town in a major hurry yesterday. Wooie! Was that a show you and Vangie's grandson put on! Where did Marlow go so fast?"

"He left town." Feeling a flush rising to her cheeks, she turned away to inspect a horse liniment display. "Granddad's getting married."

"I heard. Dunc called Doc and broke the good news. The whole town knows by now. Cal's oldest boy says he'll ranch-sit while you're gone."

Jessica sighed. "That helps."

"You don't sound very happy for your granddad, Jessie."

"I have to get a dress for the wedding."

"Oh. And wear it too, I suppose, eh?"

"Wipe the silly grin off your face, Pete. You know I wasn't born to shop."

"You shop for tack and hay and feed okay. A dress can't be much different."

She scowled. "You've never worn one, Pete. Or high heels, either."

"Well now, you're right about that. What can I help you with in the way of tack and feed?"

"Nothing. I just came in to put off pawing through the dress racks."

"You might as well get it over with," Pete advised kindly. "Call up Betsy. She'll help you. I suspect she's an expert at dress shopping."

Jessica had to agree. "Thanks for the advice."

"I've got one more piece for you, Jessie."

"What's that?"

"If you didn't notice yesterday, Raitt Marlow's got a big sweet streak for you."

"A big yellow streak," she corrected. "It runs straight down the middle of love and marriage."

She left Pete ruminating on a peanut and trudged to the variety store. For a small store, it turned out to have more shapes and sizes of curlers, rollers and twisters for hair than Jessica had imagined any female ever needing.

She walked out without buying anything. Who could decide? Choosing a dress had to be easier. She went into the nearer of the two clothing stores.

"Time for new 501s?" the clerk asked.

"No, only a dress."

The clerk, Rhoda, stared at her. She was Cal's wife, plump and cheery. "A what?"

"Just show me where they are and point to my size. And don't ask me what size I am or stare at me like I've gone crazy."

"Gee, Jessie. I didn't mean to. You never come in looking for dresses."

"Not plural, Rhoda. Dress. Wedding. Got it?"

Rhoda stared again. "Raitt Marlow asked you to marry him?"

"Granddad's wedding, not mine." Jessica tapped her toe impatiently. "Never in a million years would it be Raitt marrying me."

At last Rhoda looked as if she understood. "Doc Coulter wasn't exaggerating, then. Dunc *is* getting married. In Reno, Doc says. Why Reno? I ask Pete this morning. He says, 'Why not?' You know Pete, so easygoing. And then Cal puts in his two cents' worth about how Las Vegas was bigger than Reno, the last time he looked. Cal's never laid eyes on Vegas, mind you."

Luckily, Rhoda began moving as she chattered, bustling to a short rack crammed with multicolored ruffles and flounces that made Jessica certain she'd look totally unlike herself at Dunc's wedding.

Well, shopping took her mind off Raitt, so it couldn't be all bad. Maybe that was why so many women shopped till they dropped. Maybe it was the only known way to forget about certain men.

"This blue might be nice with your skin tone," Rhoda was saying as she pulled hanger after hanger out of the rack. "Hot pink is too garish. These two greens will play up your eyes. White won't do. Yellow, I don't think so. Too much mustard in this shade."

Jessica got a fleeting impression of how cattle must feel being wrangled into a pen when Rhoda rounded her up and headed her into a mirrored cubicle with six dresses.

"You'll need the right slip, too," Rhoda was chanting as she closed the cubicle door. "Panty hose, as well. Or maybe those new, lace-trimmed thigh highs that came in the other day—"

"I've already got a pair of nylons," Jessica cut in, recalling that Cal's wife never went on and on like this about Levi's.

"A single pair? What if you get a run?" Rhoda fretted beyond the cubicle door. "Betsy swears these thigh highs stay up without bagging at the knees. But then she has legs like I haven't had since I was sixteen. Lycra supposedly does wonders for cellulite...."

Jessica flopped onto the cubicle stool and plugged her ears, convinced she'd never get out of there with just a dress.

As far as she could see, shopping took forever, and the clerks never shut up.

BY THE TIME Rhoda pronounced the boat-necked, seafoam-green dress perfect, Jessica had decided never to go shopping for *anything* again. Except at the Feed-and-Tack.

Even so, she had to admit that the delicate green had a surprising and positive effect on her eyes. It had a few other positives going for it, as well.

For one, the blouson bodice made wearing a bra unnecessary. *Blouson,* was a new word for her, courtesy of Rhoda. For another, the swirling skirt and rolled hem gave it a floating, breezy quality. Strappy, midheeled sandals made her legs seem longer and slimmer.

Rhoda selected a string of iridescent, freshwater pearls and matching drop earrings as *accessories,* another unfamiliar fashion term.

Driving home in the pickup after staying far too long at the store, Jessica felt exhausted. Wrangling steers and stringing fences had never been half as wearying as preparing for Dunc's wedding.

She tried not to think how it would feel to be a permanent third wheel at the ranch after the newlyweds returned and got settled. Life wouldn't be the same—but Dunc would be happier married to Vangie. That was the important thing. Pete was right; they were a good match.

Once again, the weather report on the truck radio advised listeners that a mountain storm was brewing. Jessica hoped to reach home before it hit. She always put the horses in the stable during storms. Alamo, especially, didn't react to thunder and lightning with dignity and aplomb.

She'd just have to find the energy, even though hers had already been spent—on the two shopping bags she'd carted out of the store. Thank heaven, that ordeal was over. She wasn't sure yet whether she had survived.

Fat raindrops had begun to drip from dark, gathering clouds when she turned into the driveway. She carried the shopping bags to her room, then turned her attention to the horses.

She was securing Alamo in his stall and congratulating herself for patching the roof in time, when a loud crack of thunder sounded. Alamo started and rolled his eyes, but he had safely weathered a fierce electrical storm in the early spring without injuring himself, so she wasn't overly concerned about this current upset.

Fortunately, the other horses were more even-tempered, not so prone to losing their cool if they were in the stable, enclosed in their familiar stalls with enough feed and water. Aunt Lucille had been known to doze and even snore during storms. Cody seemed unperturbed.

Jessica left the stable, followed by Murph and Muttley. Halfway to the house, lightning flashed so brightly that she had to fling her forearm over her eyes to shield them from the searing glare. She heard tree branches above her cracking and tearing away from the trunk. Dry, sharp pine needles hailed down.

"Murph! Muttley!" she shouted, pointing to their dog door at the back of the house. "Go!"

They hesitated, cowering as tree limbs came crashing down around them.

"Go!"

Murph obeyed and streaked through the door, followed by Muttley. There was a deafening clap of thunder, and Jessica covered her ears. She stumbled toward the door, tripped on a fallen branch and fell to the ground.

A massive limb landed in front of her, blocking her path. She struggled to her knees, saw a flash of flame, then heard more of the broken tree thud to earth behind her.

Lightning sizzled high in the sky. More thunder racked the air.

"Raitt!" she heard herself cry. That was senseless; he was gone. Gone for good. She was on her own now. Lurching to her feet, she took a step.

She heard another fir limb tear loose above, saw it plummet toward her.

"Raitt!" she screamed again. Then everything went dark.

12

"JESSIE?"

Jessica heard a faraway voice repeating her name and struggled to open her eyes. Someone seemed to have hung heavy weights on them. A hand was patting her cheek, squeezing her arm. She smelled wood smoke and pine pitch. Her clothes felt wet.

"Jessie, can you hear me?" The voice was pleading, growing clearer, louder . . . a woman's voice . . .

"Can't shop now . . ." she mumbled. "No . . . no more thigh highs."

"Jessie, open your eyes if you can."

"No more 'cessories . . . no . . ." Jessica struggled to do what the voice asked. "No blousons. . . ." Fireworks seemed to be going off inside her head.

"I'm here. You're going to be fine, Jessie. Doc Coulter is on his way."

The weights were rising, rising, growing lighter and lighter. Jessica looked up and saw three faces looking down—Murph, Muttley, and a plump, round face that made her think she'd never finish shopping for a dress, no matter how hard she tried.

"Oh, thank God," said Rhoda, smiling tremulously.

Murph and Muttley whined and the sound registered painfully in Jessica's head. "What...happened?"

"Lightning struck the big pine out back, Jessie."

"Where am . . . ?" Jessica looked around and found she was lying on the kitchen floor under a thick quilt. A pillow was under her head. Rhoda was kneeling at her side with the dogs.

"I dragged you in and called Doc." Rhoda frowned. "Are you hurting, Jessie?"

Jessica tried to think, but nothing seemed very clear. "My head aches."

"A falling branch beaned you, I think," Rhoda said. "You have a big bump on your skull."

"I'm soaking wet, too," Jessica added, comprehending more as she regained consciousness and grew alert.

Rhoda nodded. "I put the fire out with the garden hose and doused you, too." Tears filled her eyes. "If I hadn't come by right when I did . . ."

"Fire?" Jessica struggled to sit upright, recalling a flash of flame before everything had gone dark.

"It's all put out," Rhoda assured her. "The rain helped drown it, coming when it did, right after I got you inside. A summer downpour."

Jessica became aware of rain drumming on the roof, running off the eaves. She propped herself on one elbow and regarded Rhoda with consternation. "Why are you here?"

"Because of your pearl earrings. Somehow I forgot to put them in the bag before you left. I didn't want you to make a special trip because of my mistake, so I made the trip myself. Now I'm so glad that I did. The fire had almost reached you when I got here."

The full impact of what could have happened hit her. "Sheez. Thanks, Rhoda."

"Lie back down," Rhoda ordered firmly. "Doc said you mustn't move until he gets here. It shouldn't be much longer."

Feeling too dizzy to argue, Jessica lay back upon the pillow. "How long have I been out?"

"Almost an hour. I've been scared to death, hoping you'd revive. You shouldn't be out here all alone, Jessie. Things happen that can't be predicted. I was barely strong enough to pull you inside."

Dunc's words came back. *Jessie-gal, you need a man.* Now she couldn't scoff or prove him wrong. She hadn't been able to take care of herself. Mother Nature had delivered a walloping blow.

"It might have been days before someone dropped by," Rhoda added, shaking her head. "Raitt Marlow or someone should have been here."

"There'll be Granddad and Vangie here after the honeymoon," Jessica pointed out.

Rhoda looked slightly dubious. "Doc Coulter says Dunc talked about splitting time between here and San Francisco when he called. That would make sense for Vangie, especially."

"Granddad didn't say anything about splitting time to me," Jessica said, frowning. Everything seemed to be moving out of her control—nature, Granddad, her personal independence. If Rhoda hadn't forgotten the earrings and come to deliver them . . .

The dogs ran to the door, barking, and Rhoda heaved a big sigh. "Doc's here."

He hurried in, his poncho dripping rain. "How's the patient?" he boomed. "Conscious, I see."

"Hi, Doc." Jessica managed to smile.

"Hi, yourself." He knelt and peered into her eyes, taking her pulse at the same time. "Reasonably alert. Can you tell me who you are, where you live and what day this is?"

She took a deep breath and rattled off those statistics and more, identifying Rhoda and the two dogs, then naming the five horses in the stable. "And you're Junius A. Coulter, M.D.," she added with certainty.

Doc grinned at Rhoda. "Good work, Nurse."

"Good fire fighter, too," Rhoda said, buffing her nails proudly on her collar. "The flames were licking at Jessie's shirt when I blasted them with the water hose."

Doc gave Jessica a stern look. "You could have been in a world of trouble out here, all alone. When Dunc hears what—"

"Don't you dare say a word to Granddad. Not until after he's married."

"I guess bad news would alter the wedding mood the wrong way," Doc conceded reluctantly. "Let's sit you up here and see how much damage is done."

"Granddad isn't to know about this, Doc," Jessica insisted, coming to a sitting position with his help. "If he calls either of you to shoot the breeze, you're not to tell him."

"If you aren't hurt badly, I'll keep it to myself, Jessie."

"Me, too," Rhoda promised. "The only thing I noticed is a big lump on her head, Doc."

Doc felt for the lump and examined it. He frowned at Murph and Muttley, who were licking Jessica's hand. "What are you two doing in my operating room?" He pointed under the table. "Lie down where you belong."

Heads hanging, the dogs obeyed. Looking at them, Jessica remembered ordering them through the door. A few steps more and she would have been safe, too. What if they had been knocked senseless, along with her?

What if, what if?

"What burned, exactly?" she asked Rhoda, as Doc rummaged in his black bag.

"Just one big branch near where you fell. The whole tree could have caught and gone up, too. But then, I suppose the rain would have put it out before long."

"Doc," Jessica said, "I'd like to get up from the floor, if you don't mind."

"I do mind, Jessie."

"But Alamo may have hurt himself in his stall. I've got to go out and—"

"You've got to stay put until I shine a light in your eyes and check you out. I'll say when you can get up, if you don't mind."

"But, Doc—"

Doc turned to Rhoda. "If Jessie puts up any more arguments, phone up Dunc and tell him what happened."

"Do what he says, Jessie. I'll run out and check the stable for you in a few minutes."

"Whatever you say, Doc," Jessica muttered, crossing her arms over her chest and submitting.

"Since you're arguing already with everyone in sight," Doc said, "I predict a quick recovery. By the way, if you could use a laugh right now, I thought to bring a video cassette for you from Betsy. She titled it 'Butt's End,' just for you."

Rhoda burst out laughing and Jessica had to join in.

Doc chuckled, and the skin around his eyes crinkled. "Laughter. The best medicine I know, bar none."

He continued his examination and finally decided that she seemed to have simply been knocked out cold. His lingering concern that she might have suffered a concussion resulted in Rhoda offering to stay overnight.

"I'd love a night away from Cal and the boys," she said. "Count me in."

Before Doc left, they played the tape and cracked up watching it. Seeing Raitt, Jessica's eyes grew misty, but she pretended to Rhoda and Doc that her tears were simply the result of laughing too hard.

After Doc left, they had an early dinner and a fine time viewing the tape over and over. Rhoda relished running it in slow motion during the beer bath portions.

Watching Raitt play his part, Rhoda patted her heart and panted, "My hero. I've never seen anyone look that much like the Marlboro Man."

"Except that Raitt doesn't smoke," Jessica pointed out, trying to keep her tone neutral.

"My hero twice over, then. What a hunk." Rhoda rolled her eyes. "You had him here to look at full-time, lucky girl." She grew thoughtful. "If he had been here today..."

"You did everything he could have done, Rhoda. I can't thank you enough."

"Think nothing of it. I'm just glad I forgot the earrings." Rhoda focused on the TV screen again. It showed Jessica pouring the second beer in excruciatingly slow motion. "After what Budd did to you, how did you ever get up enough courage?"

Jessica shrugged. "I'll never know."

The next morning, however, she found herself thinking that Raitt had had a lot to do with what she'd done. If he hadn't given her a healthy measure of confidence, she might never have been able to turn around ten years of humiliation within ten minutes. Whatever his motivation, Raitt had desired her and made his desire overwhelmingly evident.

She had marched into the tavern after a spectacular night with Raitt. After a spectacular fight with him, as well. She simply hadn't been the same woman Budd had known.

The next day she hired Rhoda and Cal's teenage son to do the chores while she was in San Francisco, and didn't object when Rhoda suggested that the boy should start learning the routine right away.

He and his boom box arrived that day and occupied the tack room. Jessica put him to work, clearing the scene of the fire, then started to worry about *him* being alone at the ranch. He asked one of his school friends to share the job with him and promised to check in with his parents three times a day while she was gone.

On Friday she packed a bag with her blouson dress and accessories, waved goodbye to the boys and left for San Francisco.

She had learned the hard, humbling lesson that no woman is an island. It was beginning to seem just as likely that no man was, either.

FRIDAY AT NOON, Vangie's house was busy with the comings and goings of friends and relatives. Every extra bedroom was taken by someone involved in the wedding. One party of Patton relatives was even camped in the backyard.

Raitt was taking a break from the lunchtime crowd by half watching baseball on cable TV in Vangie's tiny den, when Dunc approached and hovered in the doorway. Seeing him toss a videocassette from one hand to the other, Raitt clicked off the set with the remote control.

"This game's a dud so far," he told Dunc. "What's the video you've got?"

"Somethin' Doc Coulter sent in the mail with no word about it." Dunc frowned and read the label. "'Butt's End.' Looks homemade—and sounds like a triple-X porno to me. Maybe he thinks I'm havin' a bachelor party tonight."

Recalling Betsy and the camcorder, Raitt kept a straight face with great effort. "This is your last full day as a single man," he said, "and I qualify as a bachelor. Close the door and roll the party tape."

"*Bar* the door, you mean," Dunc muttered, stepping inside and turning the key in the lock. "If any female in this place walks in and catches us, we're mincemeat."

Raitt got up and drew the curtains. "Put it in the VCR. I haven't seen a skin flick since I worked vice during my rookie year."

"You'd better not arrest me for my last bachelor party, boy," Dunc said, loading the cassette into the player. "Or Doc, either, for sendin' the party favors along. That son of a gun."

"Yeah. He's a pistol," Raitt agreed amiably, stretching out on the couch and aiming the remote.

Dunc settled into an armchair and propped his feet up on an ottoman. "Put the sound way down so nobody out there can hear the high points."

"Right," said Raitt. He flicked the sound button to Silent and started the tape. "Party, party, party."

"What the hell!" Dunc exclaimed when the picture portion came on after the grainy leader. "What's Cal's tavern and Jessie doin' in the picture?" He gave Raitt a disappointed look, then sat back in his chair. "That's no heavy breather, no way."

Raitt clicked on the sound. "You'll get a charge out of it anyway, Dunc."

Dunc frowned at him. "What makes you say that?"

"I'll tell you later. Just watch."

Dunc rolled his eyes. "Shoot. I was all set to sin for an hour and repent later." He aimed a sharp glance at Raitt. "You stop grinnin' at me, or I'll set your mouth straight for you."

"Trust me, Dunc. You'll get a charge from this flick."

"Charge, hell! Doc's home movies are snoozers."

"Stop snoring," Raitt said. "There's Budd Cochran."

"Budd?" Dunc stared, then snarled, "That skunk." He tilted himself toward the screen like a bull ready to charge. "What's he doin' back in town?"

"Losing at stud poker. That's me behind Jess."

Dunc blinked. "Hellfire, boy, what are you doin' in the picture?"

"Enforcing the law." Raitt pushed the Pause button. "Jess got her revenge against Budd the day I left. Betsy Newman filmed it with a video camera."

"Well, I'll be!" Dunc began to chuckle as the tape continued, then roared with laughter when Budd got his beer bath. Flopping back into his chair after the tape ended, he wiped his eyes with his shirt sleeve.

"That was choicer than any bachelor party peep show I've ever watched. Run it from the start again."

Laughing along with Dunc, Raitt rewound the tape and played it through a second time.

Dunc whistled and hooted at Jess's grittiest lines. "You can say that again, gal. Holy Moses! Look at her pourin' suds to Sunday all over that mud weasel. Look at you twistin' his slimy paw."

The end came with Cal's call to drinks. Dunc clapped Raitt heartily on the back. "Thank you kindly for makin' him crawl."

"The least I could do, Dunc."

"Gal handled herself like a thoroughbred."

"Yes." Raitt had to clear his throat of the gravelly feeling he'd gotten from seeing Jess. He'd been missing her so much; too much to deny it to himself.

"Why didn't you tell me the Butt Cockroach story, boy? Hottest news in town, and I don't hear it till it's a week old."

"I knew you'd get the news one way or another."

Dunc extended his hand. "Put it here, cowboy. You didn't do the damage I would've done to Budd, but that's just as well. I'd be in jail now for manslaughter if I'd been around when he showed his varmint face."

Raitt gave Dunc's hand a firm shake. "Jess did all the advance work. I just finished him off."

"She was somethin' rich, that gal," Dunc marveled proudly, "givin' him that two-beer bath. Then you muscled in at just the right spot."

"I couldn't let him hit her, Dunc."

"'Course you couldn't." Dunc was silent for a moment. "You mind tellin' me exactly why you're not my hired hand anymore? Haven't had a chance to squeeze it out of you with all the folks comin' and goin' here."

Raitt shifted uneasily. "Jess and I can't seem to get along. That's all."

"She shouldn't be up there all alone, boy, and you shouldn't be down here, from what I can see. The other day Vangie says to me, 'Raitt acts like he's pinin' away for someone at the ranch.' I sure enough had already noticed the same thing."

"Dunc, Jess made it clear she doesn't want me up there for the next six months. Not on *my* terms, at any rate."

"What terms does she have in mind?"

"Longer than six months."

Dunc nodded. "Like the permanent terms I'm takin' up with your grandmother tomorrow. The whole bowl of chili."

"Exactly. Jess is a one-man-forever woman. Not my type."

"Raitt, you got anythin' like love in your heart for that gal? Tell me true."

Raitt got up and began pacing, hands jammed in his pockets. "She argues with me constantly. Once she gets her heels dug in, there's no digging them out. At the tavern, after Budd, I thought she might...but no, she wouldn't. I told her 'no strings' right from the start, and I never stopped saying it."

"You weren't expectin' to fall face flat in love, were you, lawman?"

"No." Raitt stopped in midstep. "I mean—"

"I see all the giveaway signs," Dunc cut in, waving a hand. "Nobody falls in love without it showin' like a neon light. Question is, what do you plan to do about it?"

"There's nothing to do, Dunc. You've met my parents and all of my stepparents. Look what they've done. Made a mess of their lives."

"Yep. None of 'em looks straight at each other or has a good word to exchange among themselves. But you've met most of Jessie's side of the family, just the opposite. You've taken a real likin' to the Patton side."

Raitt couldn't disagree. Meeting Don and Beth— Dunc's son and daughter-in-law—and getting to know them at Vangie's, had been a pleasure he hadn't anticipated. Jessica's younger sister was no different. Robyn and her husband, Keith, were as vibrant, charming and as happily married as her parents. Their two young children were adorable.

The members of his own family were tense, guarded, occupied with avoiding each other at every opportunity, whereas the Pattons were happily crowded together in Vangie's house. He was drawn to them. It was a pleasure to give them his delighted attention, his growing affection, and he knew he'd miss them after they left.

"You've seen what marriage can be these past few days," Dunc said, rising from his chair. "I hope you've seen it can be worth a try, if the two people are right for each other, like Don and Beth are. And Robyn and Keith. And Vangie and yours truly. And maybe you and Jessie-gal."

The doorknob jiggled and a knock sounded. "Dunc?" Vangie called. "Are you in there?"

"Yep. Raitt, too."

"Why is the door locked?"

Dunc winked at Raitt. "We're havin' a bachelor party."

"A what? Speak up."

Dunc opened the door. "Raitt's educatin' me. Tellin' me all the facts of life and divorce."

"Oh, Raitt." Vangie frowned, looking disgusted. "How can you even think we're making a mistake by getting married? You're making the mistake, letting Jessie slip through your fingers. I'm so happy to become part of a happy family. You could, too, you know."

Don and Keith squeezed into the room past Dunc and Vangie. "Is that ball game still playing?" Don asked.

"Duncan," said Vangie, "no baseball for the groom today. Come pay attention to the bride." She led him away.

Raitt clicked on the set. "Still playing. Have a seat." He sat down to watch with Don and Keith and immediately started to enjoy their company.

Jess was all that was missing. He had never missed a woman this much. Never more than now, in the midst of her loving, lovable family. Since she resembled each of them in one way or another, all he could do was think about her.

"Jessie should be here soon," her father remarked, "if she left the ranch when she said she would."

Raitt covertly checked the time. The second hand on his wristwatch had never ticked so slowly.

13

JESSICA PARKED Dunc's pickup in the closest empty space, halfway down the street from Vangie's house. She could see her parents' car among the many that lined the curb in front. There was Robyn and Keith's station wagon, parked behind a cousin's convertible.

There was Raitt's red sports car.

She breathed deeply and got out of the truck. Vangie's street was lined with trees on both sides. The lots were small, the houses compact and bay-windowed in the San Francisco style. A very nice neighborhood, Jessica surmised as she glanced at the tiny, trimmed front lawns and neat shrubbery.

San Francisco's famous fog was nowhere to be seen; in fact, the day was sunny, breezy and warm. Dunc had mentioned on the phone last night that they were having a heat wave.

"Wear a sundress," he had commanded. "The pink one."

As if she had any other dress in her closet—besides the new one that he'd never seen, of course. Ignoring his gruff order, she had not worn the pink one, though she had brought it along. Instead she wore a sleeveless, knit top, clean jeans and sneakers.

Her one concession to him was to wear her hair down instead of in her usual ponytail. He'd be pleased about that, if not about the jeans.

No telling what Raitt would think.

She pulled her heavy suitcase out of the pickup and started to lug it down the sidewalk to the house. Seeing Raitt come out, she slowed.

"I'll get that for you," he called from the front steps.

"I can handle it," she countered. "Don't bother."

"You're not my boss lady anymore, Jess," he said, reaching her and forcing the suitcase out of her grip. "On my own turf, I'm the boss."

He stood looking at her, apparently unmoved, and she found it impossible to meet his blue eyes. She focused on his belt buckle. Wrong spot. On his chest. Wrong again. His chin? Another mistake. Every inch of his tall frame and handsome face had a memory attached to it.

"Before you go in, you should know that Doc Coulter sent Betsy's video to Dunc. The adults are watching the show right now."

"I've seen it already."

"Quite a performance, Jess." A grin tugged at the corners of his mouth. "You could end up with an Oscar nomination."

Now she looked into his eyes and felt her heart leap. "So could you." *My hero.*

Her suitcase in one hand, he turned and took her elbow in the other. "Let's go in. Don and Beth are anxious to see you. Everyone is, except the divorced

Marlows in the crowd. They're too busy hating and avoiding each other to pay attention to anyone else."

"That mustn't be comfortable for Vangie and you." She tried to control her reaction to his warm touch.

"The atmosphere is tense," he agreed, "but they're curbing their worst hostilities out of respect for her and for the occasion. Irreconcilable differences and counter communication are the family way."

She went up the front steps with him, thinking aloud. "The same can be said of our own relationship."

"We're talking, at least," he said with a shake of his head. "They aren't. Ignore the chill they give off, if you can."

Jessica hesitated at the door. "If you're on the outs with anyone in particular, it would help me to know who beforehand."

"Just with you," he murmured, squeezing her elbow. "No one else."

"For Granddad and Vangie's sake, don't make a big thing of it, Raitt."

"I won't, if you won't," he replied, handing her through the door.

In the hubbub of Patton relatives greeting her arrival, there wasn't time for Jessica to think anymore about Raitt. She was swallowed up in hugs and kisses and enthusiastic reviews of her starring video role.

"No pink dress, gal?" Dunc scolded, then beamed his approval of her hairdo and gave her a big bear hug. Vangie stood at his side, waiting her turn.

Raitt watched Don, Beth, Robyn and Keith embrace Jessica in Vangie's long living room. He glanced from his own mother, who sat at one end of the room with her allies, to his father at the opposite end, surrounded by Marlow supporters. Both of them were now legally separated from their most recent spouses.

Fortunately, the Pattons formed a warm buffer between the two cold-war camps.

He caught Vangie's attention and pointed to Jessica's suitcase in the entryway. "Where shall I put it?"

Vangie took him aside. "In your car."

"What?"

"There isn't an inch of extra space here, Raitt. You have a sofa sleeper in your extra bedroom, as I recall, so Jessie will be most comfortable with you."

"Look, Jess and I aren't—"

Dunc came up and interrupted. "Where do you want Jessie's suitcase to go, Vangie?"

"Raitt has kindly offered room for her at his place," said Vangie, smiling sweetly at her grandson. "He does owe two Pattons for hosting his stay at the ranch when I visited."

Dunc clapped Raitt heartily on the back. "Even trade, boy. I'll leave Jessie's luggage to you."

"Jess won't agree," Raitt warned. "No way."

"Duncan will persuade her," she said, kissing her fiancé's cheek and leaving a bright red lipstick print on it.

"Am I wearing that kiss, Miss Vangie?"

"Yes, and I kind of like it there. It brands you as Vangie's property," she teased. "Go tell Jessie the good news."

Dunc went off to do that. Raitt turned on one heel and sought the refuge of the den and the sports on TV. There he found Robyn's little boy and girl watching cartoons.

"Mind if I join you?" he growled.

They were too wrapped up in Captain Planet either to notice him or answer, so he hunched in front of the TV with them and waited to hear Jess explode.

JESSICA WAS TELLING one of her cousins something about Alamo when Dunc tapped her on the shoulder.

"'Scuse me," he said. "How would you like to know where you can unpack later and settle yourself for the night? Come along with me."

"I probably should get that dress onto a hanger before too long," Jessica mused, following him upstairs. "Rhoda swore any fold wrinkles would hang out overnight."

Dunc led her down a hall, pointing to rooms left and right. "Vangie's room there, Robyn and Keith in this one with the kids, Don and Beth next door to 'em, and mine at the end." He motioned her into his room and closed the door.

She looked around expectantly. "And me where?"

"Raitt's got a nice sofa sleeper for you."

"Raitt?" She almost choked.

"Yep. You two got some makin' up with each other to do. No better place for it than his condo."

"Granddad, I've never heard such a ridicu—"

"Bite your flappin' tongue, gal, and hear me out. Vangie's house here is stretched to the limit. We've got kin campin' in tents out back and hammocks hangin' from the basement beams."

"I'll find a motel, then."

"Not right now, with the American Medical Association convention takin' up every room for a hundred miles around. No, ma'am. And don't think you'll bunk in my truck on the streets of Frisco, either. Nope."

"Raitt's place can't be the last resort," she insisted.

"Well now, that's what he says too, but this is Vangie's and my weddin'. The bride and groom get to have things any way they want. You and Raitt can have your way when *you* get hitched."

"That'll be the day," Jessica scoffed, "when Raitt Marlow gets married."

"Stranger things than that happen in the natural world, gal. I don't want to hear 'boo' again about where you stay, you hear? Put on your guest manners and don't take 'em off until you head back to the ranch."

"Yes, Granddad. It's your wedding, not mine."

He curved a comforting arm around her slumping shoulders. "Won't be long before it's your big day. You'll see. Your prince will come shinin' through for you. True love always shines through."

There was a knock on the door. "Dunc?" Vangie's voice. "May I come in?"

"Yep. Help yourself."

She opened the door, looking worried. "The restaurant just called. A water pipe burst in the banquet room we reserved for this evening's dinner, and now they can't serve our group, period. What do you think?"

Dunc frowned and thought for a moment, then brightened. "Home-delivery pizza?"

"Hmm." Vangie perked up. "Where could we get that many pizzas at one time?"

"Let's order a half dozen from each of five or six places. That won't overload anybody's circuits."

"Duncan, you dear, brilliant man. I'll put Raitt to work, phoning the ones that deliver. It's probably all for the best, anyway. Everyone can relax, eat early and get a good night's sleep."

"And won't have to dress up," Jessica added, glimpsing the only silver lining in sight.

"Has Dunc told you about the room shortage, Jessie?"

Guest manners. "Yes. How kind of Raitt to help out in a tight pinch."

"Isn't he a prince?" Vangie waved and disappeared.

"Not *my* prince," Jessica murmured.

Dunc's eyes searched hers. "Do you wish he was, gal? Tell me true."

"Yes," she said after a long moment, "so let's change the subject. What made you think of pizza out of the wild blue yonder?"

"I reckon it's the necktie I would've had to wear to a fancy restaurant."

Jessica had to smile, then to laugh. "You're too much."

He winked. "That's what Vangie says between the sheets."

"RIGHT, six Monster combos," Raitt said into the den telephone. "No anchovies."

It was his last pizza order. Everything was falling into place for their impromptu home dinner on the eve of the wedding. Someone had been dispatched to buy wine, soft drinks and plastic glasses. Someone else was out getting paper plates and napkins. Beth was using the neighbor's phone to notify those not present of the change in dinner plans.

Raitt didn't know where Jess was, but was wondering why he hadn't heard fireworks yet.

"That's right. Deliver them to 799 Capwell Place at six o'clock tonight. Thanks."

He hung up and stared at the phone, remembering that pizza was a certain street kid's favorite food.

Vangie hovered in the doorway. "All systems go?"

He nodded. "Since dinner will be casual, would you mind if Tim Waverly joined us?"

"Call him immediately," she agreed, then blew him a kiss and flitted away.

Raitt dialed the number of the group home where Tim lived. Luckily, he was there.

"Yeah, yeah, yeah," the boy said when Raitt said, "pizza at my grandmother's house."

Raitt was giving him the address and directions when Jessica walked in, carrying two whiskey glasses. He finished the call, then commented, "I hope one of those is for me."

"One for you," she confirmed, handing him a glass. "One for me. Both Jack Daniel's, neat. Cheers."

"What's the occasion?"

"Your kind offer of a room for the night. I assume you had no more to say about the setup than I did."

"Probably less," he said with a wry smile. "I don't argue half as much as you do."

She sat down on the couch with him and didn't argue, proving him wrong, for once. "Are you working at a desk yet?"

"Not yet. I start after the wedding." He took a short swig of his whiskey. "How is Cody doing?"

"Fine." She sipped from her glass, then shook her head. "What a forced, stilted conversation we're having. A lot like the Marlows I've been getting to know out there."

"Yeah. If I ever had a wife, she'd have terrific in-laws, wouldn't she?"

Wife? "I'm growing to like Vangie very much, Raitt."

"You'll grow to love her, Jess." He stared into his drink. "I've had a great time with your side of the family these past few days. They're so . . . happy."

"Happily married, you mean," she said. "They're pretty high on you, too. When did Robyn's kids start calling you Uncle Raitt?"

"The day they got here. I rode them around on my shoulders, you know. Stuff like that." He looked up from his drink. "I've really been missing you. Ever since I left the tavern."

Jessica swallowed hard. "I've missed you, too, ever since I said 'Good riddance.'"

Raitt got up so quickly that Jessica jumped. He locked the door, then stood with his back against it, looking at her. Holding out his arms, he beckoned.

"Come here, Miss Jess. Kiss me hello."

She covered the distance in a heartbeat, hurtling into his embrace. Home. It felt like home in his arms. Safe. She hadn't felt safe since the storm. Raitt. She loved him so much.

Her emotion and need flowed to him through her kiss. He drank it in thirstily, taking possession of her soft, yielding lips, revealing his own raw feelings and rampant desires.

He couldn't get enough of her, knew he'd never get enough as long as he lived. Hope surged in him as he held her, a hope he'd never had before.

Framing her face in his hands, he covered it with fervent kisses. Sliding his fingers into her dark, silky hair, he cradled her head and kissed the succulent depths of her mouth.

And as his fingers stroked erotic circles over her scalp, they came across a hard bump. Raitt pulled slowly out of the kiss, looked down and measured the egg-shaped swelling with his fingertips. Alarm swelled in his eyes.

"What's this?"

She rested her cheek against his chest and regained her breath. "It's a lesson I learned the hard way."

"How? When? God, Jess, you got hurt after I left?"

"I'm fine now." She stroked his cheek to relax his tightly clenched jaw. "Let's sit down and I'll explain."

He swung her into his arms and settled on the couch with her on his lap. "You got hurt after I left," he repeated, a frown furrowing his forehead.

Safe in the protection of his arms, Jessica explained about the lightning storm, the fire and Rhoda.

"I should never have walked out on you," he said after she finished. "I left you all alone."

"Raitt, I could have hired a replacement that same day. I didn't. My own foolish pride put me at risk, not your leaving me alone. Now I know I can't rely totally on myself. I should never have thought I could."

He pillowed her head upon his shoulder and stroked her hair. "You could have died."

"Fate saved me."

"*I* should have saved you. If I'd been there, we'd have stabled the horses together. We'd have headed for the house together. We might have even been safe in bed."

She nodded. "Together."

"Jess, I've been a fool, too. I was falling in love with you, but—"

"You were?" She lifted her head.

"I still am," he said miserably. "It won't stop. It quit being friendly sex along the way and got to be more than I could handle."

Jessica traced his jaw with one fingertip. "I fell in love, too, cowboy."

Drawing his head down to her own, she offered him a tender, loving, clinging kiss. She offered him her heart and the feminine softness she had discovered in herself. In a single kiss, she surrendered to him what she had never relinquished to any man before, the power and the glory of her true love.

She didn't stop kissing him and wouldn't stop until he gave up his deepest emotion in return, in full measure, in trust for the future.

Raitt's misery evaporated. His head, his senses reeled. He felt Jess's warm fingers curl around the back of his neck, sensed the sweet, silent invitation to give her his heart and stake his claim to hers. He felt himself accepting, clasping her tight, allowing her to chip away the stone wall he had erected against things like love and commitment.

She was so warm, so giving, her love so gently insistent. She was the one woman he had to have. He had to have her all to himself, had to claim the hope she was opening up to him, for him, in him.

"Make love to me, Raitt," she whispered against his lips.

"Now," he agreed huskily. "Here. Yes."

He moved, she moved, and elemental need had them lying down on the couch in no time. Buttons seemed to free themselves, clothing to slip aside. He touched and tongued her breasts as he uncovered them. She caressed and kissed his nipples in turn, her soft murmurs feathering the hair on his bare chest.

He drew down the zipper of her jeans. She undid the buttons of his.

A knock at the door. "Raitt?" Dunc's voice. "Tim Waverly's here."

14

JESSICA STAYED IN THE DEN after Raitt had gotten his act together and gone out to greet Tim.

She wasn't certain whether to feel doomed or ecstatic. Raitt had actually said he loved her! What ecstasy to know that, to hear him say each word! But he hadn't said one word about anything beyond that.

She had felt safe and secure in his arms, wise and womanly. She had felt as if he truly loved her—enough to want her in his life for ever and ever. For the first time in her life she had felt beautiful. Her heart was still soaring.

Her little niece and nephew wandered in. Sean was six and Sara three. Both were brown-eyed and blond, like their father, Keith.

"Can we watch cartoons, Aunt Jessie?" Sean asked.

"Sure." She handed Sara the remote control. "You both look a little bored."

"There's too much grown-ups and not enough kids," Sara complained, clicking the TV to a cartoon featuring Darkwing Duck.

Sean settled on the carpet to watch, but Sara lost interest immediately. She climbed into Jessica's lap to hug and cuddle.

"Sara, you're growing into such a big girl."

"I know. I'm getting big as Sean."

"Are not," Sean muttered, without moving his eyes from Darkwing.

"Aunt Jessie, what's plane?"

"Plane is short for airplane. Planes fly in the sky."

Sara looked perplexed. "You're not a airplane."

"Well, of course I'm not. I can't fly."

"Raitt's uncle said you are. He said 'plane as a potato.'"

"Oh." *Plain*. Raitt's uncle was only a little less handsome than Raitt, with gray-gold hair and eyes nearly as blue.

"Can potatoes fly, Aunt Jessie?"

"No." Her soaring heart crashed and burned to a cinder. Reality was more brutal than it had ever been. It drew hot, stinging tears to her eyes.

Plain as a potato. She had to get outside and breathe fresh air. She would never be beautiful like Betsy, never pretty like Robyn, never the stuff of a man's dreams.

When sexual attraction began to wane, what would Raitt see? The same thing his uncle could plainly see. What everyone else saw whenever they looked at her, unless they were blind.

"Mashed potatoes are the best," said Sara.

Jessica knew just how such spuds felt. Beaten up. Mashed to a pulp. Squished and squashed and squelched.

Raitt appeared in the doorway. "Jess, come on out to the backyard. Tim wants to meet my girlfriend—and Sean and Sara, too."

"I'll be along in a minute," she said, forcing the words past the tight knot in her throat.

The kids scrambled up and followed Raitt out the back door. Staring at Darkwing through a blur of tears, Jessica thought about slipping out the front door and driving back to the ranch. Horses and cattle and chickens didn't know plain from potato.

That was where she belonged, where she needed to be, with or without Raitt. She stood, aimed the remote at Darkwing and blindly clicked the control.

It didn't stop. *Wrong button.* The VCR began to whir. "Butt's End" began to play at the halfway point of the tape. Through her tears she saw herself triumphing over Budd, over her own humiliation, over the woman she had once been.

She saw something else, too. Raitt at her side. Raitt stepping forward. Raitt helping her triumph.

At that moment she saw a way to triumph over the plainest fact of her life.

"SO DO YOU have a girlfriend or not?" Tim asked Raitt in Vangie's noisy, crowded backyard.

"Yeah," Raitt replied. He shifted in his lawn chair and glanced at his watch. "She's coming . . . eventually."

"You said that ten minutes ago, dude." Tim looked around. "Her sister's a cute babe."

"Woman or lady," Raitt corrected sternly. "Not 'babe.'"

"Just a figure of speech."

"Clean up your act, or you'll be odd man out when the Monster combos get here. Furthermore, if you aren't a perfect gentleman toward Jess, you'll answer to the law."

"I'll be nice, man. If she ever gets here." Tim hunched into the collar of his black leather jacket. "What's holding her up?"

Raitt couldn't imagine that she was primping or waiting to use the bathroom. Everyone was outside right now. His father in one corner of the yard, his mother in another, all the Pattons in the middle. Sean and Sara were playing dodgeball against the fence.

Tim pointed at the back door. "Is that her?"

"Yes." Raitt smiled and motioned. "That's—" He broke off, seeing her go toward the corner where his uncle was sitting. She had a brown paper sack of something in one hand. She was giving it to his uncle. He saw him take the sack, open it, peer inside.

Tim sat forward. "What's in it? The dude's turning bloodred, whatever it is."

Feeling smug, Jessica turned away and looked around. The big potato and the lunch bag hadn't been too difficult to locate in Vangie's kitchen. The important thing was that they seemed to have done the job.

Where was Raitt? Ah, there he was, looking somewhat quizzical. And the boy in the leather jacket with him was—

"Dear God!" she gasped under her breath, seeing Tim clearly for the first time. For a half moment she couldn't help staring.

He had brown hair, gray eyes, and a large, port-wine birthmark that stained most of his face.

She felt her own face flush as she went to them and sat down in the empty lawn chair Raitt had saved. She shook Tim's hand as Raitt introduced him to her.

"Raitt didn't warn you, did he?" Tim said, raising one eyebrow.

"No," she admitted. "I'm sorry I reacted."

Tim smiled, shrugged. "Everyone goes goggle-eyed the first time. I've gotten used to it, mostly."

"I was just surprised."

"Raitt says I'm marked for special things. I say he's full of road apples." He gave Raitt a challenging glance. "See, Officer Marlow? I'm cleaning up my four-letter mouth. Cody would be proud of me. How's he doing?"

"Ask Jess. She saw him last."

"Cody's just fine," Jessica responded. "He and my mare, Teardrop, have become quick friends."

"Teardrop," Tim repeated, looking thoughtful. "Is she a sad horse?"

"No. I was sad when I named her, actually. But then she has a teardrop-shaped marking, so the name fits."

"Raitt says your ranch is cool and you ride like the wind. 'Poetry in motion,' right, Raitt?"

A honking car horn cut off Raitt's reply. "Must be the pizzas. I'll go help. Jess, keep Tim out of trouble for the next few minutes."

Jessica saw admiration glow in Tim's eyes as he watched Raitt leave. "How long have you known Raitt, Tim?"

"Long enough to learn a few things from him. I used to hate cops. Raitt's different." He looked her frankly up and down. "So are you. I thought you'd be a knockout cowgirl babe—I mean, lady."

"Then we're both surprised, aren't we?"

"I don't know. My picture is changing. I can see you looking good in a hat and boots. And one of those leather jackets with fringes." He looked around. "I've never gone to a wedding dinner before. Is Raitt's grandma really marrying your grandpa?"

"Yes, she really is."

"Love at first sight, huh?"

"Exactly."

Jessica realized that she had stopped focusing on Tim's big, ragged birthmark. His gray eyes, so bright and inquisitive, had caught her attention. He seemed mature for thirteen, hardly the slum child she had imagined. How cruel insensitive people must be to him. There were too many in the world.

"Raitt learned—I mean, taught me to make decent conversation. My old pals rag me when I talk right."

"I wouldn't have guessed you weren't born making decent conversation, Tim."

Raitt returned and asked them to help to put the food out for everyone to serve themselves. Soon they were all enjoying pizza and salad and the warm, summer evening. The sky darkened and people started to drift inside after the meal. Vangie put on some soft music and several couples started dancing.

Outside with Raitt and Tim, Jessica heard herself say, "I'd love it if you—and Raitt—would visit the ranch after Granddad's wedding."

Tim looked surprised. "I thought visiting was out, all of a sudden."

"I didn't realize then how important it could be," she explained. "For all of us."

Raitt's face took on a guarded expression. "I'll look into it, maybe."

"Only maybe?" Tim inquired in a small, pleading voice.

"Okay, I will. But I can't get more than a weekend at a time away from the job I start on Monday."

"You can get more if you don't start the job," Jessica said in a low voice.

Raitt frowned and glanced at Tim. "It's getting late. I don't want you to miss your curfew."

Tim rolled his eyes. "The home is just ten minutes away on the streetcar."

"Jess and I will drop you off on our way home."

"Home?" Tim looked from Raitt to Jessica. "You're living together?"

Raitt cleared his throat. "I have a sofa sleeper for Jess to use. Just for tonight."

Tim grinned as if he didn't believe a word of it. "Your car will be a tight fit for all of us."

Recalling her suitcase, Jessica said, "Let's take the pickup. No one will be cramped that way."

"We'd better get gone," Raitt said, checking his watch. "Tomorrow will be a long day."

A few minutes later, after a lot of goodbyes, Dunc and Vangie waved them off in the truck. Raitt drove and Jessica sat between him and Tim. She closed her eyes and made a wish that they'd ride three abreast like this on horses, one day soon. Like a family.

"Catch you later," Tim said, hopping out when they reached the home. "I owe you one, Raitt." He paused, holding the door open. "Jessica, what was in the bag you gave that guy?"

She pretended to think for a moment. "Just a potato."

"A what?" He and Raitt spoke at the same time.

"My own private joke. Good night, Tim. I'm so glad Raitt invited you to dinner. I'll be even happier if he brings you up to the ranch."

Tim waved and ran up the steps of the group home.

Raitt turned to look at her. "You don't know my uncle well enough to share a private joke with him. He keeps his distance, even from me. What's the real story?"

"I'll tell you someday, when we're old and gray."

Shaking his head in puzzlement, Raitt pulled away from the curb. "That's a long time from now, Jess."

"We'll be in-laws after tomorrow, Raitt. Think of all the Thanksgivings, Christmases and family gatherings we'll both attend in the future."

"I've been thinking," Raitt mumbled.

Riding with Raitt in thoughtful silence, Jessica felt her heart expanding with the deeper knowledge of Raitt she had gained through Tim.

"You're wonderful with that boy," she said.

"Anyone would be. Deep down, he's a real gem. He shines brighter every day he stays off the streets."

"You're a gem, too, Raitt. A man to rival Granddad, in a lot of ways."

Raitt gave her a wary look and steered the truck into the driveway of the condominium complex. "Here we are. Leave lugging the suitcase to me, all right?"

"Fine."

"No argument? You're not acting like yourself, Jess."

"Maybe I've changed, Raitt." She knew she had; she'd changed for the better. Admitting she needed help wasn't the weakness she had once thought.

Leading her into his condo, Raitt inquired, "What's this about visiting the ranch after the wedding?"

"Let me unpack a few things and freshen up before I explain. Which room is mine?"

"That's up to you." He tipped an imaginary hat. "Miss Jess."

"Your room, then. At least for tonight."

"With me in it?"

She gave him a soft smile of agreement. "While you're giving me a minute to myself, would you pour me a drink?"

"I'll pour us both one," he said, carrying her suitcase to his bedroom and warning, "I never make my bed. My bathroom's not real shipshape, either."

She glanced fondly around at the utilitarian decor and masculine disorder. "Just as I expected. You and Granddad are a lot alike."

Raitt withdrew and closed the door. He went to the kitchen, got out two wineglasses and opened a bottle of Grey Riesling. As he poured the wine, he got the uncanniest feeling that this wouldn't be the last time he poured drinks for Jess and himself.

Vangie might just be right. Letting Jess slip through his fingers might be the biggest mistake he could make. All week he had observed Vangie and Dunc together and seen their faces glow with the joy they daily discovered in each other.

Just yesterday, Dunc had said to him, "I'm a whole man again, boy, all due to your grandmother's lovin' ways."

Raitt knew himself to be less mature than Dunc, less manly—and less loved in all the ways that Dunc was loved. Dunc was fearless about taking the big risk with Vangie, about making the vows that would bind him to her in more emotional and legal ways than anyone could count. Beyond being fearless, Dunc was eager to risk, to commit and bind himself to the future.

Jess's grandfather had a rock-solid confidence, a confidence Raitt had observed before only in his own grandfather. Until he'd met Dunc, he had felt that Vangie's marriage to Leland had been an aberration, a fluke. Dunc was proof positive that it wasn't. Dunc, a whole man.

Raitt carried the wine to the living room and waited for Jess. She joined him less than a minute later and sat down beside him.

"Mmm. Wine. Let's have a toast."

He handed her a glass and took up the other. "To what?"

"To Granddad and Vangie, of course." She clinked her glass against his. "I just realized that no one thought to propose endless toasts to the bride and groom tonight."

"Maybe because they already seem married," he ventured.

"They do, don't they?" She drank with him to their health and happiness, then set down her glass. "And now let's change the subject. To us."

He set his glass next to hers. "I've been giving that touchy subject some extra thought since I left the ranch, Jess."

"Me, too, Raitt. Especially this afternoon, after you said you loved me. Do you really?"

He took her hands and clasped them in his own. "I really do, Jess. I've flirted with love before, but never fallen more than halfway until now."

"Raitt, please come back up to the ranch and bring Tim, even for a day or two. He doesn't know it, but he made me see something about you today."

"What?"

"Something I wouldn't let myself trust in while you were at the ranch. Your inner beauty."

"Jess, yours is—"

"Shh. I haven't finished. Today I saw my own inner self as well, in a new light." She smiled. "I'll never be the knockout cowgirl babe Tim was probably expecting to meet."

"You knock my heart out all the time, Jess." Raitt clasped her hands more tightly. "And in bed . . . well, you know what you do to me there."

"I love hearing that, cowboy, but I never really believed it all until I saw Tim. Nursing my old, broken heart had gotten to be my worst habit. You once told me I didn't give myself enough credit, and you were right."

"I knew that when I said it," he affirmed. "You paid me back by rapping my own bad habits—of resisting marriage and commitment as if my life depended on staying single."

"People who really love each other work things out, Raitt."

"Are you arguing with me again?" he demanded tenderly.

"Yes. And hoping we can find a way to work things out for ourselves."

Raitt leaned forward and framed her face in his hands. "Let's start the search in my bed and see how things go from there."

He covered her lips with a hungry, searching kiss and Jessica couldn't think of any argument.

THEY DIDN'T WAKE next morning until the phone rang. Raitt fumbled it to his ear.

"Where are you two?" Dunc crustily inquired. "The buses are loaded and waiting, Reno bound."

"We'll drive up in the car," Raitt mumbled. "We overslept."

"Overslept? In one bed or two, boy?"

"Er, one."

"Boy, you've got some explainin' to do to the Patton portion of this family."

"I'll think up something plausible, Dunc."

"Think up a happy endin', where you and Jessie-gal do my ranchin' for me while I gallivant around with Vangie. Fill up that log house with street kids who need a good gulp of mountain air. Start havin' your own kids together. Git a life."

"Yes, sir," Raitt promised and hung up. He rolled over and gathered Jess into his arms, where she had spent the night.

"What did Granddad say?"

"He told me to quit the patrol, make an honest woman of you and be your ranch partner."

"Mmm." She nipped his earlobe. "Those sound like the same terms we agreed to last night—twice."

Raitt nuzzled between her breasts, murmuring, "Will you marry me, Jess? Share ranch life with me? Make the ranch a place where street kids can work during the summer?"

"You already asked me all of that last night. Twice."

"Did I tell you that it's the kids, not police work, are what's important to me?"

"Twice."

"Is your answer still the same?"

"Yes, yes, yes. But only if you promise to wear your Stetson down the aisle."

"I already promised twice last night."

"Is your answer still the same, prince of cowboys?"

"Yes, yes, yes, Miss Jess."

He didn't doubt that he'd give Dunc that happy ending. Rock solid and confident, Raitt began making sweet, slow, true love to the most beautiful woman in his world.

**Relive the romance...
Harlequin and Silhouette
are proud to present**

by Request

A program of collections of three complete novels by the most
requested authors with the most requested themes. Be sure to
look for one volume each month with three complete novels by
top name authors.

In June: **NINE MONTHS** Penny Jordan
                              Stella Cameron
                              Janice Kaiser

**Three women pregnant and alone. But a lot can
happen in nine months!**

In July: **DADDY'S
            HOME**   Kristin James
                          Naomi Horton
                          Mary Lynn Baxter

**Daddy's Home... and his presence is long
overdue!**

In August: **FORGOTTEN
            PAST**   Barbara Kaye
                          Pamela Browning
                          Nancy Martin

**Do you dare to create a future if you've forgotten
the past?**

Available at your favorite retail outlet.

HARLEQUIN   Silhouette

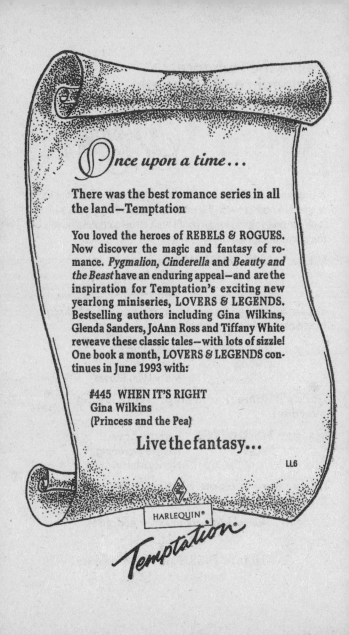

THREE UNFORGETTABLE HEROINES
THREE AWARD-WINNING AUTHORS

MAVERICK HEARTS

A unique collection of historical short stories that capture the spirit of America's last frontier.

HEATHER GRAHAM POZZESSERE—over 10 million copies of her books in print worldwide
Lonesome Rider—The story of an Eastern widow and the renegade half-breed who becomes her protector.

PATRICIA POTTER—an author whose books are consistently Waldenbooks bestsellers
Against the Wind—Two people, battered by heartache, prove that love can heal all.

JOAN JOHNSTON—award-winning Western historical author with 17 books to her credit
One Simple Wish—A woman with a past discovers that dreams really do come true.

Join us for an exciting journey West with
UNTAMED
Available in July, wherever Harlequin books are sold.

MAV93

Harlequin is proud to present our best authors and their best books. Always the best for your reading pleasure!

Throughout 1993, Harlequin will bring you exciting books by some of the top names in contemporary romance!

In June, look for *Threats and Promises* by

BARBARA DELINSKY

The plan was to make her nervous....

Lauren Stevens was so preoccupied with her new looks and her new business that she really didn't notice a pattern to the peculiar "little incidents"—incidents that could eventually take her life. However, she did notice the sudden appearance of the attractive and interesting Matt Kruger who *claimed* to be a close friend of her dead brother....

Find out more in THREATS AND PROMISES . . . available wherever Harlequin books are sold.

BOB2

Fifty red-blooded, white-hot, true-blue hunks from every
State in the Union!

Beginning in May, look for MEN MADE IN AMERICA!
Written by some of our most popular authors, these
stories feature fifty of the strongest, sexiest men, each
from a different state in the union!

Two titles available every other month at your favorite
retail outlet.

In May, look for:

FULL HOUSE by Jackie Weger (Alabama)
BORROWED DREAMS by Debbie Macomber (Alaska)

In July, look for:

CALL IT DESTINY by Jayne Ann Krentz (Arizona)
ANOTHER KIND OF LOVE by Mary Lynn Baxter
(Arkansas)

You won't be able to resist MEN MADE IN AMERICA!